CASSIE & JASPER
To the Rescue

by

Bryn Fleming

WESTWINDS
PRESS®

Library of Congress Cataloging-in-Publication Data
Fleming, Bryn.
  Cassie and Jasper to the rescue / by Bryn Fleming.
     pages cm. — (The range rider series)
  Summary: Can cowgirl Cassie and and her sidekick Jasper rescue a neglected horse from the owner's villainous son?
  ISBN 978-0-88240-992-4 (pbk.)
  ISBN 978-1-941821-03-9 (e-book)
  ISBN 978-1-941821-04-6 (hardbound)
  [1. Horses—Fiction. 2. Animals—Treatment—Fiction. 3. Friendship—Fiction. 4. Cowgirls—Fiction. 5. Cowboys—Fiction. 6. Ranch life—Fiction.] I. Title.
  PZ7.F59933Cas 2014
  [Fic]—dc23
                            2013046932

Cover illustration by Ned Gannon
Edited by Michelle McCann
Designed by Vicki Knapton

Published by WestWinds Press®
An imprint of

GRAPHIC ARTS
BOOKS®
P.O. Box 56118
Portland, Oregon 97238-6118
503-254-5591

www.graphicartsbooks.com

Acknowledgments

Thank you to everyone at Graphic Arts Books® for giving this new author a chance and to Nadine, who introduced us. This book was also made possible by a grant from the Wheeler County Cultural and Heritage Coalition in Fossil, Oregon.

Chapter 1

My horse, Rowdy, and I galloped over the sagebrush hills of our ranch. The wind whipped his mane in my face as I leaned low over his neck, urging him faster and faster. . . .

"Cassie!"

Ms. T.'s voice was sharp enough to tear a jagged hole in my daydreams. I looked up and could see the other kids smirking behind their hands. Ms. T. propped her hands on her hips and narrowed her eyes behind her red plastic-rimmed glasses. "Cassie, please stand and read your homework assignment."

I sighed, stood, and fought back an eye roll. Best not to push things *too* far. I read the title on the notebook paper in my hand: "Describe Yourself Without Telling What You Look Like."

We were learning creative writing; making up believable characters, lining up an exciting plot and all that. As if kids weren't natural-born storytellers. And liars.

I squinted at my "chicken scratches," as Pa called my handwriting, and read:

I'm a twelve-year-old girl.

I love my horse, Rowdy.

I'm going to be a rancher like my pa.

I have my own herd of two cows. They'll be old enough to breed next year, then I'll have four, more if they have twins.

That's all.

I sat down. Ms. T. pursed her lips. "Thank you, Cassie."

I almost admired her for not blowing up at me. I knew that it wasn't the kind of paper she was looking for.

"Class, what does her characterization tell us about Cassie?"

The window next to my desk leaned open a crack. The sweet smell of juniper and sage fingered its way in and tangled with the B.O. of a dozen kids and Ms. T.'s fake spring deodorant soap. I tried to sort it out and only breathe in the outdoors. It smelled like freedom.

Cab raised his hand.

"Cab?" Ms. T. called on him.

"Even though she doesn't say what she looks like, like what she's wearing, I could picture her with cow crap on her boots and a big ol' cowboy hat." The other kids laughed. Cab smiled big.

"Um . . . good, Cab." Ms. T. smiled. "That may be accurate. But what can you tell about her character, her hopes and dreams, her values and motivations?"

I was a bug under a microscope. When would this be over? These kids had never cared about my likes and dislikes, my hopes and dreams before. Why would they start now?

Stan called out from the back, without raising his hand at all. "She'll never get a boyfriend smelling like cow crap." More laughter.

I didn't care. I crossed my arms across my chest and crossed my boots under my desk. The clock above the door tick-ticked. Thirty more minutes of torture. I stared out the window.

"Okay, that's enough, let's be constructive with our comments." Ms. T.'s neck was getting pink, a flush of frustration crawling toward her face. "Jasper," she called on the scruffy kid who always sat in the back row.

"I can tell that she cares about animals," he said.

"That shows she's probably nice to them. And she's not prissy."

"Very good, Jasper," Ms. T. smiled. "What else?"

I studied the light falling through the leaves of the big locust tree on the edge of the playground. Listened to the sparrows chirp as they hopped branch to branch, wherever they wanted to go. . . .

"Yes, Carlie?" Ms. T. called on probably the prissiest of the prissies. Each of her nails was painted a rosy pink and had a little flower decal on it. Obviously, she didn't have enough chores to take up her time in the mornings. Or to chip her precious nail polish.

"She probably doesn't know how to dress, what's in fashion or anything. She probably only wears T-shirts and jeans and work stuff."

Before Ms. T. could respond, smarty Samantha chimed in: "And she probably doesn't care about education, about going to college or anything. She thinks she knows it all already."

Carlie had a point. I couldn't have cared less whether pink or black or neon green was in style. But Samantha, now that really wasn't fair. I was plenty aware that I wasn't the smartest chicken in the coop. I just knew what I wanted is all.

Ms. T. seemed lost behind her glasses, just staring

at us. She tried to steer us back. "Okay, class, I think you're getting the idea how characterization works. Sometimes you can tell a lot more about a person by his or her thoughts and behavior than by what they look like. When you're writing your stories, be sure to include both an inner and outer view of your characters."

"Arturo, why don't you read your paper next."

"Yes, ma'am." Arty stood and began to read.

I lost interest by about the third word. The light slanted lower as we crept closer and closer to that final bell. Today was one of those days I felt like there was no possible way I'd make it through another six years of sitting indoors listening to this stuff. Forget college; just get me through seventh grade, eighth grade, high school.

Was quitting an option? Pa would kill me. He was a firm believer in the power of education to give a person a leg up in life.

But right now, school didn't feel like a leg up. It felt like a giant rock crushing the breath out of me. I didn't care about ancient history or world religions or past participles or particles or whatever. I was bored to tears.

The bell rang. End of school, finally. I picked up my books and started out the door. Freedom!

Then I heard: "Cassie, please stay after class."

I watched the other kids file out, some of them

turning to laugh at me, not even hiding it now. "I'll miss the bus," I said.

"I'll only keep you a minute" Ms. T. sat on the corner of her desk now, looking at me like I was a piece of bad fruit at the grocery store. "Cassie, it's obvious that you are not applying yourself to your assignments." She took her glasses off and eyeballed me. "Do you think that schoolwork is unimportant?"

How should I answer that? I decided to go for honesty for a change.

"Actually, yes."

We both waited. The pink flush raced up her neck this time.

"Like I said, I want to be a rancher. Everything I need to know about cattle and feed and fencing and calving I learn at home. Maybe I got born at the wrong time," I stared at the floor, searching for a way to explain it. "Like I should have been a pioneer, back when you learned everything by doing it and nothing you didn't need."

"I see. So you feel like you're different and special."

I opened my mouth to tell her she had it wrong, then gave up. She didn't understand.

"Consider this a warning: I want more attention and enthusiasm out of you, Cassie, both in class and in your homework. Or I *will* call your father." She crossed her arms and stuck her chin up like she'd just won a fight.

"Now," she looked down her nose at me, "you may go."

I felt the blood beating in my ears as I dialed the combo on my locker. Great. Just what I needed. Just what Pa needed. As if he didn't have enough to worry about raising two girls on his own.

I threw my books into my locker and grabbed my backpack. My character description fell out and drifted to the dirty linoleum floor. I gave it a little twist under my foot and ran for the bus.

Chapter 2

Are you following me?" I felt a little mean, but Jasper got on my nerves. "You've been lurking around all day." I glared at him. "And I know this isn't your stop."

He'd gotten off the school bus right behind me. Now, the yellow bus rattled on up toward the C-Bar Ranch, paused, and spit out the Connelly twins at their gate. Jasper's stop was the next ranch after the C-Bar.

Jasper looked at the ground. "No, it's just," he stammered and shuffled his boots in the driveway dust.

Now, I'm not a particularly tall girl, just average, but he was a head shorter, so I looked down at his wreck of a haircut. Jasper has short dark hair and deep brown eyes. His mom is from Mexico and he looks more like her than his pop, who's from around here.

"I need your help," he finally got out. "You're the only one who can do it."

When I didn't answer, but just looked at him, he added, "I saw you running barrels at the rodeo last summer, on your paint horse."

"Rowdy," I said. "His name is Rowdy. We're going to take first in our class next time."

Jasper looked at the ground. "Yeah, well, you're really good with horses."

I remembered Jasper at the rodeo, too. He rode a little dun pony that stood stock still while he swung a rope. They took the blue ribbon for the junior roping event. He had a good, quick hand and a steady eye. I admired his riding and rope work.

I started up the drive. "I've got chores to do."

"There's a horse," Jasper said behind me, "a horse in trouble."

I turned back to him, "What horse? Where?" It burned me up to see someone being mean to an animal. What right did they have? Only bullies pick on little kids and animals.

Jasper smiled kind of sideways. "I knew you'd help."

"I didn't say yes, yet. Tell me about the horse," I pressed him. "But make it fast, I've got chores to do."

I just wanted to get done with the feeding so I could go for a ride. I started to walk away.

Jasper trotted after me up the drive. "My brother Danny had to haul a ton of hay up to this old lady's house last weekend, for her cows, and I went along to help unload." He panted, trying to keep up.

"Yeah, and?" I said as I kept walking.

"There was a horse there, circling in a round pen by the barn. All by herself, just walking, around and around with her head down."

"Nothing wrong with that," I said, "a horse walking in circles."

"Up close, her hooves were grown out long like elf shoes. You know, curled up at the toes."

"So she needs a hoof trim." I wasn't convinced of the need for interference, yet. We were almost to where the gravel drive split in a Y, one side going up to the house and the other to the barn and machine shed.

"Her backbone bumped out in little knobs," he went on. "And I could count her ribs from across the pen."

That got my attention and I stopped. I'd seen starving horses before. His description fit. I considered it. "Well, you brought a ton of hay, right?"

He nodded.

"Maybe the lady ran out for a couple weeks. It

doesn't take long for an old horse to lose weight."

"Maybe," he said. "She whinnied and leaned on the gate when we started taking the bales off the truck. I finally took her a couple handfuls."

I started walking again. We were so close to the house now I could smell biscuits baking. My sister, Fran, made biscuits almost as light and flaky as Mom's had been. My mouth watered.

"So the horse has hay to eat now and she'll fatten up again," I said, annoyed that he'd trailed me this far. "Shouldn't you be getting home?"

He took a big breath. "So here's the thing—when I did that, when I threw a little hay in her pen, this guy came runnin' out of the house and yelled at me."

"Yelled?" I wondered if Jasper was a scaredy-cat and just exaggerating.

"I don't know who he was, but he came busting out the back door so fast I about toppled over the fence. He yelled 'get away from that horse,' so I got away."

Jasper went on, his voice a little shaky, "He told me, 'That horse ain't good fer nothin' an' it don't need no food.'"

I pulled a blade of bunchgrass and chewed the stem while I considered. I always figured that if an animal ended up in my life, I was responsible for it, for loving it and for keeping it out of the weather and giving it food and fresh water. It made me sick to see a dog on a chain, alone in a yard day after day, or a litter of kittens dumped by the side of the road.

"Where do this lady and the crazy guy and the skinny horse live?" I knew just about everybody in this end of the county, at least to say "hello" to.

"It's a ways out, off Skyline, after the field with the sheep. The black ones, not the regular ones." He crinkled up his forehead. "Then up a dirt road a mile or so and then there's a fork and you stay to the left. Or maybe it was the right."

"Well," I considered, "it sounds like it might need investigating."

He smiled at that. "I can take you there to look at her. You'll see. She needs us. Maybe tomorrow after school?"

I thought about it. He'd got my curiosity up and I wanted to see this poor horse for myself. "We better make it Saturday, in case it takes us all day to find the place."

He hung his head, but looked up at me still smiling. "Aw, I can lead you right to it; I'm just no good at giving directions."

"I'll meet you under the Hanging Tree at nine on Saturday morning. You know the Hanging Tree, right?"

"'Course I know it," he said. "Everybody knows it."

"It's a deal, then," I said, putting out my hand. Jasper looked at it a second then shook it.

If I'd known then all the trouble that handshake was going to get us into, I might have turned tail and run. But probably not.

Chapter 3

"What?" I asked.

At supper that night, I'd looked up to find my big sister, Fran, staring at me as I pushed mashed potatoes around on my plate.

"What planet are you living on, Cass? Did you even hear a word I said?" Fran was a serious fifteen.

I looked from her to Pa. "Guess not." What else could I say?

"She's like this at school, too, Pa." Fran clattered her fork down. "I've heard the teachers talking in the hall. I doubt she'll daydream her way out of sixth grade this spring." It was inconvenient, sometimes, having all the grades in one school building, little kids up to high schoolers, but that's how it is out here.

"That true, Cassie?" Pa asked me. "You don't listen in class?"

"Sometimes, I guess." I shifted on my hard wooden chair. "My mind gets to chewing on a thing. . . ."

"And what are you chewing on now?" Fran asked, raising her eyebrows. "Not your supper."

I wasn't about to discuss Jasper and the horse with my family.

"Nothing important," I lied.

Fran looked at me another minute. I went back to making a mashed potato swimming hole and spooned gravy into it.

"School's important, Cass." Pa didn't sound too convincing.

"I want to help run the ranch, Pa. How does that take algebra and social studies?" It was an argument I'd made before. I knew I'd get the same answer.

"It's important to be a well-rounded person, to know a little bit about most things and a lot about some." He could get philosophical, especially toward the end of supper.

"Right," I said. "Pass the peas, please." It was usually best just to agree. And I had other things on my mind.

Fran handed me the delicate china bowl, one of the few nice dishes we hadn't broken over the years.

"Pa, do you know a ranch up off Skyline, an older lady and maybe her grown-up son? Past the sheep fields."

"The McCarthy's?" Pa's face darkened and his fork stopped halfway to his mouth. "What do you want with that place?"

"I was just hearing things about it is all." I stabbed my chop a couple times with my fork.

"You don't need to concern yourself with that place." Pa's voice was loud and tight. "That poor woman's got enough troubles with her no-good son, Carl. Plus I heard her husband died not too long ago." He pointed his fork at me, the chunk of pork chop still skewered on it. "Don't ever let me hear you've been up there. That Carl can't be trusted."

"You know him?" I asked.

Pa nodded. "The guy's been a bully since we were kids. He dropped out of school after the eighth grade, been in and out of trouble ever since."

Pa looked me right in the eyes, to make sure I got his point: bad guys don't care about education.

"I remember one time, Carl and I found a beat-up old bicycle in the grass by the side of the road. Well, it didn't belong to him any more than it did to me, but he took it. Wouldn't let me touch it. Nearly broke my arm pulling it away from me. Busted old bike with a bent wheel."

He waited until I looked up at him. "Stay away from him. Got it?"

"Yeah, I got it."

Pa said, "Well, then," and went back to cutting his pork chop. "This sure is a better tasting pig than last year's."

"Yessir," I said, though I couldn't tell one pig from another by the time it got to my plate.

Finally, Pa pushed his chair back and crumpled his paper napkin on his plate. "You did a fine job with the chops, Fran."

"Thanks, Pa." Fran did most of the cooking since we'd lost our mom two years ago. "I made apple cake for dessert."

"Mom's recipe, with lots of cinnamon?" I asked.

Fran nodded, keeping her head down. She picked up Pa's plate. We were all still raw about Mom passing. It'd only been about three years since she'd gotten sick and just a few months after that when she died.

Fran and I cleared and did the dishes together. Good way to make the peace. Dad invited us to play some rummy before bed, but I was too tired.

"You guys go ahead," I said, as I went down the hall to the room Fran and I shared.

With the door cracked open a little, I could just make out Pa and Fran talking quietly over their cards.

"Really, Pa," Fran was almost whispering, "Cassie's running wild. She doesn't listen to anyone these days. Not me, not her teachers, not even you."

"I know," Pa sounded tired. "It's hard to run the ranch and bring up you girls without your mom. Heck, it wasn't easy when she was here. And money's always tight, cattle sales are down. . . ."

"Yeah, I know. Hey, rummy on your queen," Fran said. "I want to help out more with the money; I could get a job this summer."

"We'll see," was the last thing I heard before I dropped off.

I woke up four or five times, tossed and turned when I did sleep. I kept picturing that poor, skinny horse, getting weaker by the day. And that crazy guy, Carl, maybe even beating her just for kicks.

I had to see the situation for myself. Maybe Jasper was mistaken. Maybe he hadn't heard right. But if it was true and the horse was being abused and neglected, well then we'd sure have to do something about it. Wouldn't be able to stand myself otherwise.

But what could we do? Kidnap a horse? We'd be criminals, like Carl. We'd go to jail if we got caught.

Chapter 4

The next morning, I sat astride Rowdy at the foot of the Hanging Tree. Up on the ridge I could see all the way down to the John Day River winding between hills and cliffs. I followed its route with my eyes, trying not feel nervous about what we were about to do.

I watched Jasper ride Tig up the far side of the hill toward us, the pony picking her way between the stunted junipers and gray-green sagebrush clumps.

The big black locust tree stood on a ridge between our ranches, right at the edge of the rimrock. A foot of fraying rope still swung from a strong, straight limb. If the guy on the rope had swung out, his feet would be flailing at thin air over the cliff.

Of course, no one had hung there for ages. Maybe in my grandpa's time. Horse thieves and train robbers. I had no intention of robbing a train, but horse thieving might be a necessity. I shivered a little as I watched the swinging rope.

Jasper and Tig crested the hill. Rowdy nickered a greeting to Tig and the pony rubbed noses with him.

"Do you think that's the real rope they used, you know, to hang people from?" Jasper sat on Tig next to me, and Rowdy, tilting his head back.

"Doubt it," I replied. "Who knows?"

"Here." I held out my old black hat, one I never wore since Uncle Chris gave me a new one. I'd left the blue and yellow beaded band with the hawk feather on Jasper's. A good hat could help a guy's confidence.

"Hey, thanks!" His eyes glinted from under the hat brim shade as he settled it low. He looked like the bank robber Billy the Kid.

"So? Shortcut through Kelly's field? That will put us about where you said the turnoff from Skyline is."

"Sure," he agreed.

The young oats were just starting to poke out of the dirt in their long rows, back and forth across the field. We kept to the edges so as not to trample them. We took turns hopping down to open gates through field after field, always closing them behind us.

"Seems like we've been riding a long time," I said. It had been at least forty-five minutes, maybe an hour.

"It's farther than I remembered," Jasper called from behind me.

"Next time we go on a recon mission, we need to start earlier."

"What's recon?" he asked.

"Reconnaissance, you know, checking things out, seeing what we've got to deal with."

"Oh," he said behind me, and was quiet as we rode on.

At the top of the last hill, we stopped to let the horses rest. The white line of the county road snaked through the valley below us.

We hit the paved road and followed it a quarter mile or so before we turned off. From there the pavement gave way to gravel and dirt. At a Y junction in the road, Jasper pointed to the right. "That way."

"You're sure?" I didn't want to get another mile to find out we'd taken a wrong turn.

"Yep," he said. We urged the horses into a trot.

We came around a curve where a hill had blocked the view until now.

"There it is." Jasper pointed at a sprawl of old ranch buildings cradled in the fold of some bunchgrass hills. Another dirt road spiked off toward it. A gray metal mailbox stood at the roadside by the junction. "McCarthy" it said in black painted letters.

"We better leave the horses here." Jasper and Tig followed as I rode Rowdy down a little deer trail. It cut away from the road and into a draw, out of sight of the road and the ranch. We left the horses tied to a clump of sage, nodding in the sun.

"Okay," I said as we started down the road on foot. "First step in recon: don't get caught. So, keep close together and stay quiet."

"The horse's pen is right there between the house and the barn." Jasper bit his lip.

I measured the distance with my eyes and looked for any cover we might use. "We'll follow the fence line up, and then dodge behind the barn."

"Come on, and stay low." I started off. I didn't want to give either of us time to reconsider.

A gate barred the driveway as it branched off from the road we'd been on. A short chain looped around the gate and post and a padlock glinted in the sun. I climbed over the gate, and Jasper followed.

We crouched down, following the barbwire fence line up the road. A thick swath of wild roses covered the fence as we got closer to the house. Between the roses and the sage, I was fairly sure we were hidden.

We were about halfway to the house when I heard the rattle of the lock on the gate. A truck door slammed.

I saw it from the corner of my eye; a cloud of brown dust rising on the road behind us. Gravel crunched under tires.

I grabbed Jasper's skinny arm and pulled him down behind a clump of sage. He'd heard it, too, and shot me a wide-eyed, panicked look.

A white-cabbed flatbed truck rattled closer and slowed down when it was just even with us. My stomach did a flip. Jasper's mouth dropped open. I put my finger to my lips.

Chapter 5

Dios mio!" Jasper whispered. "That's him, the crazy guy!"

Jasper slipped into Spanish sometimes, but I knew what he meant. A cold shiver ran up my spine.

So that was Carl. He must have been about Pa's age, nearly forty, since they'd been kids together, but he looked a lot older than that. Kind of worn out and used up. He wore a dark blue baseball cap and a dirty white T-shirt. His arms were sunburnt red and a black tattoo snuck down from under his sleeve. I couldn't make out the picture.

A long drooping moustache hid his mouth, like the bad guy in a cowboy movie. The cap bill made his eyes tiny black chips.

What worried me more than Carl was the black-and-white McNab sheepdog balanced on a toolbox in the back.

Sure enough, the dog turned his head right toward Jasper and me, like he was sniffing a threat out of the dusty air. He must have caught a whiff of us, because his hackles stood up on his shoulders and back. A quiet growl rumbled out of him like the start of a storm. I held my breath.

Carl got out of the cab and came around to the dog.

"What's up, boy?" He followed the dog's stare with his eyes. "Is it a coyote?" he rubbed the dog's ears a little. "Settle down. You don't need to mess with no coyote." He tilted his hat brim to shade out the sun and, as Pa calls it, relieved himself in a stream onto the dirt.

Carl looked around him one more time, his eyes passing right over us. Then he was back in the truck and rattling on up toward the house again, the dog looking back at the sagebrush that concealed us. Jasper and I let out a long breath at the same time.

We practically crawled the rest of the way up to where the pasture fence met the peeling pickets of the yard fence. We leaned against a tool shed; Jasper's eyes were bright and wide.

"It's kinda too late to turn back, isn't it?" he whispered.

"We haven't even checked on the horse yet," I said, "so, it's actually too *early* to turn back. Come on, we'll be okay."

If someone had looked out the window on our side of the house, they would have seen us running for the barn. It should have been a short dash, but it felt like a marathon, like in a dream where you just can't make any progress, your feet sucked deep into mud or sand.

Finally, we ducked behind the big red barn, out of sight of the house and yard, safe for the moment.

I eased up to the corner and peeked out. The farmyard was laid out pretty much like ours; barn, big old two-story house, a three-sided shed full of wire rolls and tools and an old tractor, a rough-shingled lean-two against the shed stacked with split firewood, and the corral.

The round corral stood between us and the house. It was made out of gray planks, some of them broken and slanting into the dirt. The gate looked sturdy though, and glinted with a chain loop around the gatepost.

A small chestnut-colored mare walked a slow circle in the dust, her hooves dragging trails through the dirt. She'd worn a rut just inside the perimeter of the pen. I wondered if she always walked this direction, or if sometimes she went the other way around. There wasn't much else to do.

She was thin, all right; her ribs like the skeleton frame of a boat and her hip bones knobbed out like a coat rack. It was a wonder she was still walking, her hooves were so long and curled. She had a raw red mark on each front leg where her hind hooves scraped every time she stepped. Her thin brown mane and tail hung in matted tangles.

My stomach turned and my heart crept up into my throat. I tasted bile in my mouth like I was going to be sick. All my life I'd felt like that, like an animal's pain was my own. Empathy, Pa called it. Extreme and inescapable empathy. Watching her stumble in slow circles, I felt caught myself: weak, tired, hopeless that anything better was coming to set me free.

I knew then for certain that we had to take the horse. Nobody else was going to lead her away from her awful life.

I didn't know the details, exactly what we'd do with her, how we'd take care of her or find her another home. I just knew in my bones that leaving her here was impossible. I couldn't look myself in the mirror if I turned my back on this horse. I looked at Jasper and his eyes said the same thing.

The white truck was parked on the far side of the yard, no driver in sight. The McNab dozed in the sun on the flatbed.

Jasper and I both jumped when the back door of the house thudded open. Carl stepped down off the little back porch, followed by an older woman wearing an apron stained brown and yellow. She held the wooden rail and took the three steps slowly. Then her watery eyes skimmed over the barnyard and I held my breath.

They stood side by side for a minute and I could see a sameness in their stance, shoulders hunched a little, heads cocked a bit to the left. Their mouths were both thin and straight. This must be his mother, Mrs. McCarthy.

Carl was a big man, like he enjoyed his food maybe too much. He loomed over his much smaller mother. He would surely tower over the two of us. Maybe he was harmless and fear was coloring what I saw. Still, we were going to steal his horse. And if what Pa said about him was true, he wasn't going to take it lying down.

Carl walked over to lean against the plank fence of the paddock. He watched the mare make a slow circuit past him.

A shiver worked its way up my spine. I felt like it was me he was sizing up. I could just make out his words across the afternoon air.

"You know she's gotta go, Ma," he said. "I won't have a no-good animal on this place. Besides, I can make a little money off her instead of paying to feed her." He spit into the dust at the horse's feet and the mare stopped near him, her head swinging low.

Mrs. McCarthy scowled. "How can you say that, Carl! 'No-good?' Glory was your father's favorite horse."

"Yeah, well, Pa was too sentimental." Carl turned and stared at his mother, who still hung on to the railing at the bottom of the stairs.

She dropped her eyes away from his. Her voice shook, "But he would have wanted her to live out her life on this ranch. She's only got maybe four or five years left. Can't you let her live them out in peace?"

"I've put enough money into useless things over the years. Now, I'm getting some money together, going to move on soon, start over, I think." He peered off into the distance, like he could see his bright new life, free of useless old things, shining on the horizon.

"Pa's Ole Glory is going to the ole auction next Saturday. I won't get much for her, but at least she'll be out of here. I'll stay with the boys in town Friday night, have a drink at the tavern, play some cards. I'll come by and pick her up first thing in the morning." Mrs. McCarthy was wringing her hands together, looking at Glory with sad wet eyes.

Carl turned to look at his mother. "And you, wouldn't you like to live at the rest home in town?"

"Now why would I want to do that?"

I couldn't believe what I was hearing. Jasper edged

up close to me and cocked his head, listening, too. "Zorillo!" he muttered.

"Huh?" I whispered. Now here was some Spanish I didn't know.

"Skunk," Jasper replied under his breath.

Carl seemed to soften up a little, or just pretended to. "Come on, Ma, you'll be better off in town. You can't take care of this place all alone and, like I said, I need to get scarce for a while."

"Why? What have you done now that you have to hide?" Her eyes narrowed and her voice tightened up. "And what about your father's cattle? He poured years of hard work and sweat into that herd."

Carl ignored her first question. "Pierce Holcomb said he'd take all the cows I'd sell him."

He went on, "That retirement place is real nice. They've got bingo and bus trips to the coast and a minister that comes around if you can't make it to church."

"The day I can't make it to church is the day I go to see the Lord in person," Mrs. McCarthy said. "Besides, I hate bingo. You know I don't gamble."

"We'll see, Ma." Seemed like he was letting it go for now. "Do you want me to take that check to the bank or not?"

"I'll get it," she said. She pulled herself along the handrail up the steps and disappeared into the house, probably the house she'd shared with her husband and raised her kids in.

She came back to the doorway and held out an envelope to her son. Carl looked the mare up and down one last time, spit again, and shook his head. He took the envelope and tucked it into his back pocket, then climbed in the truck.

He drove a tight circle in the gravel next to the corral and roared away down the drive. The McNab stood up on the toolbox and barked sharp and fast, staring back at the barn.

I turned to Jasper. "C'mon, I've seen enough."

Chapter 6

We ducked back across the yard, running low and fast. I wasn't as scared, now that Carl and his dog were out of sight. Still, we were trespassing and premeditating a crime, and my heart pounded hard in my chest.

I glanced at the house as we ran by. Mrs. McCarthy stood at the kitchen window, her apron held up over her face like she was wiping away tears.

It was a much shorter trip back down the road, like things had speeded up in time. The horses swung their heads toward us as Jasper and I came up the deer trail and into the grove where we'd left them.

We hadn't either of us said a word since we'd left the barn. Now, I gathered my reins and swung up, heading out for the road while Jasper still hopped along with one foot in the stirrup.

"Hey, wait up, will you?" he said behind me.

I pulled Rowdy up and we waited for Jasper to settle into the saddle.

"Kind of scary, huh?" he said.

"Yeah, but Pa says that being scared isn't a good reason to *not* do something."

"I wasn't saying we shouldn't try to save her," Jasper explained as he caught up to us. "I'm just saying, the guy is scary."

"That he is," I agreed.

We rode on in silence for a time, until we hit Skyline and crossed back into the oat fields.

"We'll come up with a plan." I said. "Don't worry."

"How about if we borrow my pa's horse trailer and get my brother Danny to drive the truck and we come for the horse when they're both gone?" Sounded like Jasper was working on a plan already.

"I have a feeling Mrs. McCarthy doesn't leave home much," I said. "And we'll have to do it at night. Maybe Friday night when Carl's gone. Remember he told his ma he'd be staying in town. And we'll just hope she doesn't wake up. So, no truck, no trailer, too noisy."

"Where are we gonna put her once she's rescued?" Jasper was a thinker, that's for sure.

"We need a barn, water, grass, and nobody else

around," I patted Rowdy's neck while we thought about it. "There's a box canyon with an old corral at the far north end of our ranch. Aw, but there's no water except when it flash floods in the thunderstorms."

Jasper threw out an idea. "How about if we take her to the animal shelter in Baker? We could say we found her on the road just wandering around."

"I think they only take cats and dogs," I said, "and what if Carl heard she was there and took her back?"

"Hey, wait! I know just the place!" Jasper got so excited that he kicked Tig's sides and the pony jumped forward. "The old Owens Ranch! It's abandoned; almost no one goes there except a few bird hunters. And it has water and everything we need. It's perfect!"

I thought about it for a minute. "You may have something there. There's a barn and a corral, a creek for water, and a decent dirt road going in."

"It's probably about five miles from McCarthy's, cross-country, anyway," Jasper added. "Could Glory make it that far in as bad shape as she's in?"

I leaned down from the saddle and plucked a seedy plume of rye grass and chewed it, thinking. "It'd be tough on her, but I think it's our best bet. There's a dirt road partway, and a trail following the creek the rest of the way, so we'd be pretty well hidden if she needs to stop and rest."

We crossed another couple fields and followed the old wagon road between the hills and up to the Hanging Tree.

In the shadow of the old snag, we swung down off the horses and sat cross-legged in the dirt.

"So, here's the plan." I smoothed the bare dirt in front of us and picked up a little stick. I scratched an X in the dust. "We'll meet right here at the Hanging Tree with the horses. We should start around dusk, so we can make it most of the way over in the light."

I scratched a square and a circle a little farther to the right. "Here's the corral and barn where she is now."

Jasper picked up another stick and made an oval a foot or so away from the others. "This is the Owens Ranch," he said.

I drew a line from the Hanging Tree to Glory's corral and then to the Owens place, linking the three together in a triangle. "It looks simple enough. We ride over, hide the horses right where we did today, sneak up to the corral, throw a halter on Glory, and lead her out."

"Wait," Jasper interrupted, "what if we get her out of the corral and the driveway gate is locked?" Clearly, Jasper had a talent for thinking of everything that might possibly go wrong.

"I'll bring wire cutters; we'll cut a gap in the fence next to the gate."

"Wow, you'd cut a guy's fence?" Jasper looked at me like I was nuts. "My dad says that's one of the worst things you can do to a rancher. His cows might get out, and that's his livelihood."

"If you're worried about that jerk and his cows, I'll bring some wire and patch it up behind us."

"Sounds good," said Jasper, satisfied. "Then we walk her to where our horses are hidden, mount up, and lead her behind."

"Rowdy's good at leading other horses, so I'll keep hold of Glory's lead rope," I added.

"And I can lead the way and open gates across the fields." Jasper was on his feet now, really excited.

"Sounds good." I smiled and said, "I think it might work." I stood up and untied Rowdy's reins from the sagebrush. "Can you get away tomorrow, to go check out the Owens Ranch, get it ready?"

Jasper caught up Tig's reins and swung into the saddle. "Sure, after morning feeding. I'll be done by eight."

"I'll meet you here a little after, then." I mounted up and trotted down the hill. Jasper and Tig headed home.

My head was racing with details of the plan: We'd have to go Friday night, when Carl said he'd be in town, the night before the auction. Today was Saturday. That gave us less than a week to get ready.

How would we get out of the house for so long, maybe all night, if it got complicated? My head swam with all the things that could go wrong. What if Glory was scared and wouldn't come with us? What if we got lost in the dark?

What if we got caught?

Chapter 7

Don't be mad at me, okay?"

It was the next morning and we were on our way to the Owens Ranch.

"Why? What did you do?"

"I told my brother about the plan. So he could help us." I looked over at Jasper riding Tig, but he wouldn't meet my gaze.

I liked Jasper's brother okay, what I knew of him. His name was Dante, but kids at school called him Danny.

"He came back from hauling a load of hay and there were two bales left on his truck. He miscounted, I guess. Anyway, I asked him, 'Watcha gonna do with that hay?' He said, 'Don't know. Why?' So I told him about the horse. He's gonna bring the hay out to the Owens Ranch today. And some straw for her stall, too."

"Can we trust him?" I scowled. "Every person we tell makes it riskier."

"Danny swore he wouldn't tell a soul." Jasper smiled. "I think he likes your sister, so he wants to get in good with you. Maybe you could say something nice about Danny to her?"

"Yeah, maybe," I considered. "Might be good to have extra help with some of the heavy work on the corral and barn."

Jasper let out a relieved sigh once he knew I wasn't mad. For the rest of the ride, the ideas poured out, all the things that we'd laid awake turning over in our minds the night before.

"I have an extra halter and a nice long lead rope we can use," Jasper offered. "And a five-gallon bucket for water."

"Good," I answered. "I can skim some oats out of a couple bags so it won't even look like I took any. That'll get us started, anyway."

"And we'll need brushes and a mane comb and hoof pick," Jasper said.

"Jeez, her hooves." I remembered the way they curled up and how the back ones hit her front legs when she walked.

"Yeah," Jasper nodded, "her hooves are a mess.

Maybe Danny can trim them. He does our horses."

"I don't know, they're really bad. We might have to hire someone, and they're going to ask questions." Now I had a new worry, as if I didn't have enough already. "I guess we'll cross that bridge when we get there."

"This might get expensive," Jasper ventured. "Who's going to pay for what? I mean, I don't have a lot of money saved up or anything."

"What about your allowance? You got something better to spend it on? More important than a life-or-death horse rescue?"

"No way," he replied, just like I knew he would.

"Good. Then I guess we see this thing the same way. We'll split it equal. And we'll both have to earn some money to pay the bills. I can mow lawns in town after school."

"I can move irrigation pipe at Mr. Casper's this summer," Jasper said.

We hit the north fence of the ranch in less than an hour.

"There it is," I said.

We sat the horses, admiring the shamble of buildings laid out in the swale below us. It looked like a toy farm that some kid had forgotten and left out in the yard.

"No one has lived here for at least thirty years," I said. "I think the bank owns it. Or maybe the government, 'cause I've never seen a 'For Sale' sign."

"Danny and I used to come here," Jasper said. "We played bank robber. That chicken coop was the jail." He pointed out the henhouse and its wire pen. "Danny used to lock me up in there and then leave. I had to dig out under the fence one time."

A two-story farmhouse with peeling white paint stood with its doors and windows drooped open. A few gnarled apple trees still grew in the old orchard to the east of the house. A huge barn loomed next to a juniper post-and-rail corral.

I could hear the creek splashing over a riffle as it rounded the little bend by the orchard. The watery call of blackbirds lifted up from the cattails and willows on the banks.

We left the horses grazing in the tall orchard grass.

"Fran and I came here, too," I said. "We pretended to be homesteaders living in the house. Fixed it up pretty nice: bluebells in a can on the table, flour-sack curtains." It was a good memory, my sister and I getting along like that. "Some hunters came through when we weren't here, though, left beer cans all over and kicked the cots and table to bits."

I headed for the barn. "C'mon. We better get to work."

The barn door was missing its handle, so we wedged our fingers under the bottom edge and pulled hard. Slowly, it creaked open. It was all dusty shadows inside. A mess.

We picked our way through rolls of old wire fencing tangled in the walkway between two rows of broken-down stalls. Wooden feed troughs still showed the chew marks of bored horses, all that was left of them now. A metal barrel, rusty and dented, lay on its side in one of the stalls.

I heard a rustling above us and turned just in time to see a huge barn owl drop from the rafters like a ghost. The owl swept over our heads and out the door behind us.

On the wooden feed bin I poked at a few owl pellets: coughed-up wads of hair, feathers, and the tiny, thin bones of mice and birds.

I brushed my hands off. "Time to get this place cleaned up."

The *kee-kee* of a kestrel sounded from the locust tree in the yard as we hauled junk out of the barn: half a rusty oil drum, tangles of barbwire, the heavy cast-iron doors and legs of an old woodstove, loops of baling wire, bent hubcaps. Seemed more like a junkyard than a barn.

By noon, my hands were stained rusty brown and covered with scrapes and cuts. We'd dragged a mountain of junk into the barnyard. Inside, the barn actually looked open and clear enough to house a horse who wasn't too picky.

"Looks good, real good." I leaned in the barn doorway and pictured Glory there, safe and sound.

"What about the corral? We might want to turn her out on nice days while we're at school." Jasper was standing on the bottom rail, his arms resting on the top.

I sighed. "You're right, that should be next." I was tired, but it had to be done. Like Pa always said; sometimes, you've gotta put your head down and push on through.

While we considered the fallen rails and rotting posts of the corral, a truck engine rumbled from up the drive. Jasper and I looked at each other.

"Sure hope that's Danny," Jasper said, as we both shaded our eyes and waited for the truck to come into view.

A battered blue Chevy pickup rounded the curve and chugged up between the corral and the barn. Bales of hay and straw made the back of the truck sink low.

"Oye, Danny! Over here!" Jasper waved.

Danny swung his legs out of the cab. He was tall and lanky, an older version of Jasper, with his same dark eyes and hair and skin. He wore his hat low, with the brim curled up on the sides. His black boots shone even in the dust.

"Hola, Jas." Danny held out his hand to me. "Hey, Cass. How's that bull working out for your pa? Ranch doing okay?"

"Yeah, everything's good." I shook his hand.

"How's your sister?"

"She's okay." I stuck my hands in my pockets.

"Well, maybe she could give me a call sometime." Danny looked from me to Jasper and back. "You know, since I'm helping you with your secret mission and all."

"Um, well, I'll ask her." I wasn't sure Fran even knew Danny.

"Great," he winked at me. "Let's get these bales off."

Jasper climbed on top of the load and rolled the heavy hay bales down. Danny and I wrestled them into the barn. The two straw bales were lighter and I grabbed one by the twine and hauled it into the stall.

Jasper toured Danny around the barn. "See, this will be her stall and we can keep her feed in this box. . . ." He rattled on. "Here's a peg for her bridle, which we'll have to buy, and there's a saddle rack that's still good."

I went on out into the bright sun. The barn owl swooped from one tall locust tree to another and settled at a distance on a limb. "You're just waiting for us to get out of here so you can go back to bed, aren't you?" I asked her. She blinked her eyes at me and scrunched down on the limb.

Danny had an arm on Jasper's shoulder when they came out of the barn. "You guys did a good job."

"Oh shoot, I forgot . . . we need tools. A hammer and wire cutters." I don't know why Danny made me nervous, but he did, just a little.

Danny pulled a battered metal toolbox out of his truck bed. "No problem. I came prepared. What's next?"

"The corral," Jasper answered.

Danny stood at the gap where the gate should have been. "Yeah, it wouldn't hold a sheep right now, let alone a horse. But we've got plenty to work with." He kicked a stout old rail.

We tackled the broken-down fence. Jasper and I held the rails in place while Danny hammered in new nails. We worked our way around the old corral like that, one section at a time. I liked this kind of work where you could see your progress, see things come together from stray pieces.

It took all three of us to drag the big metal water trough from the barn to the corral.

"I hope it still holds water," Jasper said.

"You'll be hauling a lot of buckets up from the creek to fill that thing," Danny looked skeptical. "You could borrow my pump every week or so, if you want, run a hose to the creek and fill the tank."

I had to admit that Jasper calling Danny in on the project was getting to be more and more helpful. I sure hoped it didn't backfire on us. Would he rat on us if Fran didn't want to go out with him?

"Well, that's Part One of the plan: the stall and corral are ready," I said. "Hope the rest goes as well."

"What's the rest of the plan?" Danny asked. I looked at Jasper and didn't say anything.

"Oh, I get it," Danny laughed as he packed his tools into the truck, "Better not tell me too much in case the law gets ahold of me."

"Pretty much," I said. "This isn't a joke to us, so don't tell *anybody anything,* okay?"

"Yeah, yeah, my lips are sealed." He laughed again and then caught my eyes and stopped smiling. "Really Cassie, you can trust me."

Danny rattled back up the drive and disappeared around the bend, a ghost of brown dust trailing him.

I looked around, amazed at all we'd done, at the mess we'd turned into almost a real ranch again. A bubble of pride swelled in my chest. Glory would be comfortable and safe from Carl. Jasper and I would spend all our free time here, away from parents and teachers and the kids at school.

As we walked back to our horses, I turned and caught sight of the owl flying back through the hayloft window into the shadowy barn. Glory's barn.

Chapter 8

All that week, the week up until the Friday night mission, Glory galloped round and round in my head, churning up my thoughts like mud. I saw her bony ribs, her hips protruding, saw her stumble over her grown-out hooves.

I pictured Carl dragging her into a trailer and off to the auction. No one would want her for a riding horse, probably not even a pasture pal for another animal. She'd probably get sold to the meat buyers for dog food. I tried to shake the pictures out of my head.

Sitting in American history class, I tried to concentrate. At first, I followed along in the book while Mr. Hardy read aloud in a flat, slow voice. Something about the Louisiana Purchase, then all I heard was blah, blah, blah . . . and then I was back at the Owens Ranch.

Instead of Mr. Hardy, I heard the kestrel *kee-kee* and the owl hoot and the *whoosh* of her wings over my head. There was a lot to figure out: could we actually sneak Glory out of her pen and over all that distance to the Owens Ranch in the dark? What if the old horse couldn't even walk that far? What if somebody saw us taking her? Would they call the sheriff or just come after us?

And we'd need to be out all night, what with getting Glory away from her ranch, leading her to the Owens Ranch, and getting her settled. How in the world would I get out of the bedroom Fran and I shared without waking her up?

The third period bell jangled me out of my seat.

Jasper was waiting by the shop building. We sat a couple feet apart on a flat rock wall and rummaged through our brown paper lunch bags.

"Want half my tuna?" Jasper held out a badly smooshed sandwich.

"I'll pass, thanks," I said. "If there's one thing Fran's pretty good at, it's packing lunches."

I set the items from my bag on the wall next to me: a can of mixed fruit complete with a plastic fork, two slices of leftover pizza from the weekend, wrapped in foil, a nice crisp Fuji apple, a grape juice box, and two brownies.

I handed one of the pizza slices and a brownie to Jasper.

"Thanks!" he said. "So, I've been thinking."

"Me, too." I chewed the cold pizza.

"We need to get out of the house for the whole night on Friday, right?" Jasper picked the pepperoni off his slice and popped it in his mouth. I nodded.

"How about if we camp out at the river? We could set up a tent and all that." He was talking faster, getting excited. "I know my folks will let me. They love it whenever I want to do outdoorsy boy stuff. Even if it's with a girl."

"That just might work," I said, feeling good about it. "Part One of the plan is done: the Owens Ranch is ready for Glory. Part Two: get permission to camp on the river. Somewhere not too close to home so nobody comes to check on us. Maybe down at Mule Shoe or Oxbow. On Friday, we'll ride down after chores and set up camp. Then, we can come and go as we please."

"Part Three: get Glory out." Jasper threw his tuna sandwich in a high arc over his shoulder into the overgrown grass behind the wall.

"Part Four: lead her to the Owens Ranch." I popped open my can of fruit.

"Part Five: mission accomplished!" Jasper grinned as he took a big bite from his brownie.

"You know," I smiled at him, "I think we might actually pull it off." It was amazing what a good solid plan could do for your confidence.

Monday afternoon dragged by; English, then PE. Just at that time of day when you want to stretch out under a tree and take it easy, there we were kicking up a slow trail of dust as we jogged around the track circling the football field.

Jasper was in my squad in PE. Us seventh graders had PE three times a week. When he came huffing up behind me, I slowed down.

"I'm sure I get plenty of exercise forking out stalls and throwing hay off a flatbed every day and all weekend, don't you?" Jasper panted.

"I'd guess all us ranch kids do." I brushed a sweaty strand of hair back behind my ear. "They should only make the town kids take PE."

"Yeah," he grinned, "that'll happen."

When we passed the parking lot, Danny waved from his truck.

I glanced toward the gym to make sure the coach wasn't looking. Ms. Strasser was chatting with one of the high school girls and had her back to us.

We veered off the track and jogged over to Danny's truck.

"Hey, Jas. Hey, Cassie," he said, smiling down at us. "I thought I might have heard from Fran by now. Did you tell her I asked about her?"

I couldn't look him in the eye. "Um, actually, I forgot. I'm really sorry. I'll do it tonight."

"Yeah, that'd be a good idea." Danny had lost his friendly smile. "This horse rescue of yours is supposed to stay secret, right? You wouldn't want me to forget, too, would you?"

Jasper's mouth fell open. "You wouldn't, Danny!"

Danny just shrugged his shoulders. "Looking forward to hearing from your sister, Cass." He slapped Jasper lightly on the back and said, "See ya, hermanito."

We stared at him as he drove off, then walked slowly back to the track and started jogging again.

"What if Fran won't have anything to do with him?" Jasper's voice shook.

"Let's cross that bridge when we get there," I said. "I'll talk to her tonight."

Ms. Strasser blew her whistle and we all turned toward the gym like cattle heading for home.

"Don't forget," Jasper said as he turned into the boys' locker room.

I nodded. With Glory's life on the line, how could I forget?

Chapter 9

That night I started pulling all the strings of our plan together.

Pa came in the back door and washed his hands at the sink. I was already setting the table for supper, putting out our three nicest plates (the blue ones with the rooster design) and the fancy ceramic water pitcher. Might as well try to get on Pa's good side.

As we were finishing dinner I explained how Jasper and I wanted to camp at the river on Friday. "We want to do some fishing, mostly, catch some trout or bass." I knew Pa thought highly of catching your own supper. "We'll cook the fish over the fire; maybe roast some potatoes in the coals."

"That sounds real good," Pa said. "My brothers and I used to camp out for weeks every summer. And in the fall, deer season, we'd pitch a tent up in the mountains and just live off the land." His eyes had gone glassy and faraway, remembering. "I may just have to stop by for some of that trout. Where are you planning to camp?"

My heart skipped a beat. "Um, we thought maybe down where Pole Creek comes in. Or maybe at Whitter's Hole. We're not sure yet. Got to scout it first."

"Good thinking," said Pa as he picked up his newspaper. That meant the conversation was over. He'd said "yes"!

It was almost too easy. He wasn't likely to check up on us. Friday was his card-playing night at Mr. Cuddy's. Most of the local ranchers went, both men and women.

Now it was my sister's turn. "Dinner sure was good, Fran. Thanks for cooking."

She smiled across the table at me. I hoped I wasn't laying it on too thick.

"Hey, do you know Jasper's brother, Danny?" I asked innocently.

She raised her eyebrows at me. "Well enough. He used to go out with Corrina before she moved. She talked about him a lot."

"Yeah, well, he asked me about you. I think he likes you." It was a lame attempt, I knew. I would have been a lousy matchmaker.

Fran squinted her eyes at me. "How do you know? Did he say he's going to ask me out?"

Pa put down his paper. "He's too old for you, Fran." Pa wasn't used to his oldest daughter dating yet.

"He's only one year older." Fran didn't usually argue with Pa. Maybe Danny had a chance after all. "I'm not even sure I would go out with him. Corrina said he was boring."

So much for Danny's chances.

"Boring?" Pa replied. "I like the sound of that. Why don't you give him a try?"

"Very funny, Pa."

This was going nowhere. I decided to push it. "Call him, Fran, please, so he'll stop bothering me."

"I'll think about it," she answered vaguely. But I could tell she was interested.

There. I'd kept my word. Whatever happened next was out of my hands.

Pa and I cleared the table and cleaned up, since Fran had cooked. It was the way we'd worked it since Mom died. Whoever cooked usually didn't have to clean up. Sometimes Pa fixed dinner, usually Saturday or Sunday. I preferred to get up early and make biscuits and gravy for breakfast a couple times a week.

After I'd finished washing up the last of the supper dishes, I ran to the barn to organize my camping gear. Tent, sleeping bag, lantern, cooking pan. I'd get the food supplies after school tomorrow. Everything was coming together.

"I'm going to do my homework and go to bed," I called when I came back in.

Back in our bedroom, I didn't get much studying done, at least not much schoolwork, but I studied the plan plenty. I went through each phase and made little notes in my spiral notebook: HALTER / LONG LEAD LINE / APPLES / WEAR DARK CLOTHES / WIRE CUTTERS . . . stuff like that.

I really was tired because I fell asleep sitting right there on the floor, leaning against my bed. I dreamed I was at the Hanging Tree. But Jasper wasn't with me— I was alone. Then someone was slipping a rope over my head muttering horse thief. Suddenly my neck cricked at a painful angle and I startled awake.

I climbed into bed and pulled the covers up to my chin. I tried to shake the creepy dream from my head, but it took a long, long time.

Chapter 10

The next morning, I grabbed an apple from the bowl on the kitchen counter. I chomped it down while I forked hay down from the loft.

"Rowdy, come here buddy," I stood at the corral fence and held the apple core on the flat of my hand for Rowdy to nibble.

"Don't worry," I told him, "you'll always be my number one horse. Glory just needs our help."

I finished chores, shouted "Bye" to Pa and grabbed my backpack full of unfinished homework.

When I swung down into the bus seat next to Jasper, the first thing out of his mouth was, "Well, is Fran going to call Danny?"

"Good morning to you, too," I sassed. "Well, it wasn't easy, but it sounds like she might." It was the best

I could do to reassure him. "Let's just concentrate on the plan. We'll just have to trust Danny for now."

On the ride to school, I showed him the list I'd made and we talked about new details. Everything was falling into place. A current of excitement coursed through me when we talked about the rescue, the paths we'd follow leading Glory through the darkness to safety. Jasper's eyes were bright.

As soon as we pulled in front of the school, I shut up. The other kids, loud and shoving, jostled us along the bus aisle and out the doors. We spilled out and dispersed like a herd of colts let out of the barn after a long night.

Another slow morning sitting through social studies, current affairs, and biology. At least biology was interesting. I'd need to know some biology to run the ranch, that was for sure.

Things went bad in Ms. T.'s English class that afternoon. I was staring out the window at a fat squirrel teasing a crow under the locust tree.

I half listened to the story Celeste had written, something really awful about a princess who gets thrown off a horse and a knight who shows up just in time to save her from a broken neck. It sure didn't improve my opinion of princesses.

"Let's pause there, Celeste. Cassie, would you please comment on Celeste's characterization? Do you find her protagonist believable?"

Now I knew she was picking on me; of all the people who could comment on Celeste's characterization, I was least qualified. I mean, really, I was barely listening.

"Well," I began, stalling for time. "To start, I don't think anyone over the age of seven is interested in stories about princesses getting rescued by knights. We're middle-schoolers, not preschoolers."

I could see Celeste's face had gone entirely pink and Ms. T.'s mouth was hanging open. I should have stopped there, but something had broken loose inside me.

"And what kind of a rider falls off her horse in the middle of a meadow?" I went on. "Did the horse step on a rattlesnake or break a cinch or what? No, she's trotting through a meadow and just falls off. Totally unrealistic."

"That's enough, Cassie. Those are not constructive comments."

But I couldn't stop, any more than the princess could stop from falling off that darned horse. "I think anyone who owns a horse ought to know how to ride it, don't you? That princess is a grade-A moron, if you ask me."

"That's enough, Cassie!"

"At least I wrote a story," Celeste yelled at me. Her

face was all blotchy and her eyes were red, like she was about to cry. "Where's yours, Miss Smarty-pants?"

"Yes, Cassie, what is your story about?" Ms. T. said, giving me a look that would kill a coyote.

Uh-oh.

I stared down at my writing journal. The journal I should have been writing in last night when I was planning instead. "Um, I didn't finish it."

I couldn't look at Celeste, but I was sure she was beaming now. I heard kids around the room snickering.

"Cassie, I'll see you after class," Ms. T. said.

When the bell rang, I stayed at my desk tracing a saddle onto my writing journal. The other kids filed out. Jasper was the last to leave and rolled his eyes and smiled at me before he disappeared into the hall.

Ms. T.'s silence swam thick and sour around us. She sat down on the desk next to mine and hunched over me like a vulture.

"I've had enough, Cassie. You are insolent, inattentive, and disruptive." She took off her glasses and peered at me. "You're also smart and creative. You have what it takes to excel in school, but I'm afraid you won't even graduate if you keep this up."

I almost said, "So what?" but kept my mouth shut for once.

"I'm going to have to call your father and discuss your behavior with him."

"Please don't call him," I begged. "Please! I'm really sorry, Ms. T. I'll do better, I promise."

"I'm sorry, but I'm afraid it's too late for that. I just don't believe you're sincere, Cassie. You don't seem to value your education at all." She shook her head and pinched the bridge of her nose, rubbing where her glasses pressed little red dents. "No, I'm afraid it's time for me to speak with your father."

"Yes, ma'am," I answered automatically. But inside I was screaming *No, no, no! Not now! This is the worst time to get in trouble.*

I moped onto the bus and sat next to Jasper. He looked worried.

"What happened, Cass?"

"Ms. T. is gonna call Pa!" I was mad now that it had sunk in. "I'll get grounded for sure. No camping trip." I shook my head. "I don't even care that much if she calls him. I can handle it. But just not now. Not until Glory's safe."

"Crap," Jasper whispered. "What do we do? How are we going to get out Friday night?"

"I don't know. Maybe she's just bluffing. Or maybe she won't call until next week." I mustered up a smile. "Let's just wait and see."

Chapter 11

The phone rang that night at seven-thirty, sharp.

I about jumped up out of my chair, where I sat diligently slogging through my homework. My stomach lurched and my heart beat faster.

I held my breath while Pa answered, "Hello?"

I stared at my history book without seeing any of the words. Then Pa laughed and said, "Sure, Tom, I can help move those cows." Phew! It was just our neighbor.

Maybe Ms. T. *was* bluffing and wouldn't call after all. The phone didn't ring again that night. When I was sure it was too late for a teacher to call, I went to bed.

Wednesday morning Jasper moved his lunch bag off the seat as the bus driver eyed me in the rearview mirror. "Take your seat, please," the driver said.

I sat down and the bus pulled away from the driveway. The bus engine growled deep, like it hated its job, carrying all these kids back and forth.

Jasper got right down to business. "Did Ms. T. call?"

I smiled big. "Nope. We're still good."

Jasper heaved a sigh. "That's great; I knew she was just trying to scare you." He slugged me in the shoulder. "I got good news, too. Mostly. Mom was all for us going camping. She said she'd had enough of roughing it in the army, but she's glad I like it. Dad, not so much."

"But he came around, right?" I nailed Jasper down with my eyes.

"Well," Jasper chewed his lip. He looked younger when he was worried. "I think maybe my dad is going to call your dad and make sure it's all okay. I won't find out until I get home this afternoon."

I thought better of pouncing on him. It would only make things worse. I took another route. "I guess that adds a little more excitement, huh?" He looked way more worried than excited right then. "It'll be okay," I told him. "My pa will talk him into it. Ms. T. won't call. Everything will work out."

Who was I trying to convince?

Jasper's forehead still had deep furrows, like a new-planted field. "It's just, well, even if camping works out, I'm pretty nervous."

"I know," I said, looking down at the lunch bag in my lap. "Me too." It felt good to admit it. "But Jas, we're going to do it. We are. We can't back out now. Besides, being scared is okay, as long as you don't let it stop you from doing the right thing."

"Yeah," he agreed. "It's almost like a mission. If we don't do it, who will?"

"Nobody," I said, "nobody else is going to save Glory."

For the rest of the bus ride, we hammered out the details in low voices: who would halter Glory and who would hold the gate, the quickest route to the Owens Ranch, how easy (or not) it would be to travel in the dark.

We took up the planning again at lunchtime, but something felt wrong. Jasper wouldn't look me in the eye as he ate his peanut butter and jelly sandwich. Finally, he stopped chewing and looked at me. "Are you sure about this, the rescue? I don't want to go to jail."

I couldn't believe what I was hearing.

"Of course I'm sure. We talked about all this, Jasper. I thought you were good. We can't leave her there, right? And we have a good plan. We're not going to get caught."

Jasper didn't answer. But the look on his face . . . he was trying to back out! "Jas, don't get chicken on me now!"

"I'm not chicken," he protested. "I just don't want to get in trouble. If we get caught, we could go to jail."

"But we're not going to get caught. Who's going to catch us? Carl will be with his buddies in town. Our parents won't expect us to be back from camping until later on Saturday."

All he said was "Umm . . ." I was afraid I'd lost him.

"Please!" I sounded desperate. "Think of Glory. What if that was Tig in trouble?"

The bell rang, so we gathered up our bags and trash.

"I gotta think about it, Cass," Jasper said, walking away from me.

"I'll see you on the bus." I called, but he was gone.

Well, seems like just when you relax and things are falling into place is just when they start to fall apart.

I fretted through classes all afternoon. For the first time since we'd started on the plan, Jasper and I sat apart on the bus ride home. I smiled at him when I got off at my driveway, but he was looking the other way. I couldn't believe he might back out.

Could I do it on my own?

Fran and Pa were gone when I got home, so I hung around the kitchen, waiting for the phone to ring. If it was Ms. T., I wouldn't answer.

Halfway through a piece of cherry pie, the phone rang. Caller ID said it was Jasper's house. I was just about as nervous to pick up as if it had been Ms. T.

"Hello?"

"I'm in," he said.

"Whew!" I let out the breath I didn't know I'd been holding.

"When I got home and was feeding Tig, I realized there was no way I could leave Glory to starve. Like you said, what if it was Tig in trouble?"

"Oh, thank you, Jas!" It was like a wet hay bale had been lifted off me. "You'll be glad, I promise. It'll be a great adventure."

"Claro," he answered in Spanish, "sure thing." I could hear the grin in his voice.

"And the camping trip? Can you go?"

"Yep," he said, relieving my other worry. "My dad talked to your dad and then I sealed the deal by promising to do extra chores for a week if he would *pleeeeeaaaase* just let me go."

We talked a little more and then hung up. The phone didn't ring again that night. Still no call from Ms. T.

Finally, I could relax a little. The rescue was going to work, I just knew it. I pictured Glory safe at last. Maybe Glory was just the beginning. Maybe someday we'd have a sanctuary full of rescued horses grazing on rich green grass, healthy and happy.

Chapter 12

Thursday. Day before the rescue. School flew by. I went over and over the preparations in my head. It felt like we were really ready. Everything was coming together.

After school, I got my camping gear out: tent, sleeping bag, flashlight, jerky, and a jar of Fran's home-canned peaches. I piled it all by the back door.

I was ready to go.

In the middle of dinner, the phone rang. I jumped in my chair and my stomach tightened around my pot roast.

Pa wiped his mouth and put his napkin by his plate. "I'll get it."

"Hello. Yep, this is him." Pa's face hardened as he listened to the voice on the other line. The pot roast felt like a rock in my belly as I realized for certain who it was. Pa glared at me as he walked with the phone into the living room. I tried not to think about what might be coming.

"So, Fran," I twirled some spaghetti around my fork, "you gonna call Danny?"

"I don't know why you're so interested, Miss Nosey, but actually, I already did. We're going to the movies on Saturday night."

"Wow, that's gr . . ."

"Cassie, come in here." Pa was standing in the doorway.

I swallowed and stood up slowly.

In the living room, Pa sat down heavily on the couch, like all of a sudden he was made out of lead. I sat in the light green armchair across from him. Mom's old chair.

"That was your English teacher, Ms. Tsuchigamo. She's really concerned about you."

"Ms. T. Yeah, I know," was all I could say.

He went on, "She says you're distracted and inappropriate in class. You don't do the assignments. You sass back."

Seeing him there, so sad and heavy, I was beginning to feel pretty bad.

"I know you don't see the use of school, Cassie, but you have to believe me: without it, life is so much harder."

"There are plenty of ranchers who never graduated from high school," I said. "Mr. Larsen quit after sixth grade to help his pa run their ranch."

"That's true, but he didn't have a choice. You do," he said with a sigh.

I'd expected anger, not this kind of tired sadness.

Pa stood up and ran his fingers through his hair. "I don't know, Cassie. What would your mother say?"

My stomach turned. What *would* she say? "I'm disappointed? I expected better from you, Cassie?" She was gone. I felt tears welling up in my eyes, then slipping down my cheeks.

I hung my head. Shame washed over me. "I'm sorry, Pa. I'll do better."

"Really, Cass? 'Cause it seems like I've heard that from you before."

"I know, Pa, but I will." I was full-on crying. Pa stood beside me now. He put an arm over my shoulder. "I'll listen in class and do my assignments. From now on."

I hated to see him so disappointed, so alone in raising us girls without Mom here to help. I didn't want to be the cause of his troubles. And I didn't want to mess up the rescue.

Pa was quiet for a minute. "I'm glad to hear that, but I'm afraid I need to put my foot down this time. You're grounded, Cassie. No riding until your schoolwork and behavior improves. And no camping trip tomorrow."

"What? No!" I panicked. The plan. The rescue. It was all going to pieces.

"Please, Pa. Please!" I begged.

Pa's eyes looked watery. I hadn't seen him cry since Mom died. "That's all I have to say about it, Cassie. Now go put your camping gear away and finish your homework. All of it." He turned his back on me and walked into the kitchen.

So that was it. No camping trip. No rescue. The plan was ruined!

Or was it?

I lay awake that night and tried to see through my anger and disappointment to a solution. There had to be a way. We were too close to give up now.

Chapter 13

Of course, I had to tell Jasper the next morning. It was Friday, the day we were supposed to go camping. That night we were supposed to rescue Glory.

"I messed up." I got it out right away, as soon as I sat down next to him on the bus.

"What do you mean?" He gaped at me.

"Ms. T. called and told Pa. He's furious. I'm grounded, no camping trip."

"What? So no rescue?" He was practically shouting at me. "After you've been talking me into it!"

"Shhhhh!" I looked around, but the bus was so noisy that no one was paying attention. "I didn't say the rescue was off. Just a glitch is all."

"Yeah? So what are we going to do?" Now Jasper sounded less angry and more worried.

"I thought about it all night. You keep on like we're still camping and I'll sneak out and meet you at the Hanging Tree." .

I said it matter of fact, like it would be easy as pie. But I wasn't so sure. Could I really sneak out without getting caught? How would I get out of the house? How would I get out of the room I shared with Fran? But these were details I'd have to figure out later. Time to get the Plan back on track.

"Really?" His eyes were wide in disbelief. "You'd do that? Dios mio! You are going to get in so much trouble."

"Only if I get caught, right? Besides, it can't be helped." I rode the wave of determination that came over me. "That horse has to be rescued and we're the ones to do it. I don't care if Pa grounds me until I'm eighteen, as long as we save Glory."

Jasper smiled and shook his head. "You're very brave, amiga. Braver than me."

I fidgeted through my classes, even chewed my nails a little. I got excused to use the restroom nearly every hour. Butterflies banged around in my stomach.

Before I knew it, I was getting off the bus at my house, waving to Jasper as the bus pulled away.

He was going to set up camp right after chores, just like we'd planned. I'd meet him at ten o'clock at the Hanging Tree. Somehow.

At dinner, seemed like no one was going to let me forget that I had messed up in school. Fran frowned at me and practically threw the saltshaker at me when I asked for it. Pa stirred the remnants of his anger around on his plate.

I didn't even pretend to be hungry.

"May I be excused?" I asked halfway through the world's most awkward meal.

"Chores, homework, and bed," Pa said. "No TV, no phone."

"Yes, sir." I carried my full plate to the kitchen and left it on the counter. I'd come back when everyone was done and help clean up.

In the barn, I brushed Rowdy. He sensed my nervousness about the rescue and sneaking out later, my sadness at disappointing Pa. He kept nibbling my shirt and rubbing his head against my chest.

"It's okay, boy." I rubbed his neck. "You and me and Jas and Tig are going to do something good tonight. Something exciting, an adventure."

I know that an animal you feel real close with can read your mind, so I sent my horse a mental picture of the rescue. I held an image of the sad skinny mare, Glory, in her corral, of Jasper and I sneaking in on foot while he and Tig waited in the junipers. I pictured all of us moving quick and quiet through the night to the Owens Ranch.

I think Rowdy got the picture, because he snorted and danced around, like he was excited to get on with it. I felt him there beside me as a partner, someone strong and brave I could count on. I was going to need all the help I could get.

I finished brushing him and oiled his tack so it wouldn't squeak as we were making our late-night getaway. I arranged the saddle and bridle in the front of the tack room, where I could find them in the dark.

I forked hay into the wheelbarrow and wheeled it out to my two black cows in the pen behind the barn. I topped off their water trough with the hose.

I climbed up to sit on the top rail of Rowdy's corral, away from the house lights where I could make out the first stars starting to poke through the darkening sky.

A coyote *yip-yipped* a couple hilltops off to the east. I breathed in the sage and dust and freedom of the night. If things went bad, I'd lose all this. Was it worth it? I knew the answer.

I couldn't sit still for long. I went back inside, finished the dishes Fran had stacked on the counter, and went to pace in my room.

Chapter 14

Nine twenty. Was Fran ever going to go to bed?

I quit pacing and lay on top of my quilted bedspread with my clothes still on: a black shirt and dark jeans, so no one could see us in the dark. My books were piled around me. How was I going to get to the Hanging Tree by ten? Would Jasper wait if I was late?

Finally, Fran came in and changed into her nightgown: nine thirty. I breathed a silent sigh of relief. Maybe I'd make it after all. Rowdy and I could make it up the hill to the Hanging Tree in ten minutes in the daylight. In the dark? I'd never tried.

"Looks like you really mean it this time," she said, eyeing the stacks of books and papers on my bed.

"Yeah, I do. I'm finishing a paper for history, then I'm going to read two chapters for biology."

She climbed under the covers and switched off the light on her nightstand.

"Good, Cass, I'm glad you're taking this seriously. Pa doesn't need anything else to worry about."

"Sure," I said. I turned back to my paper and kept writing.

I heard Pa use the bathroom and go into his own room down the other end of the hall. His door clicked shut. He never read in bed, so I knew he'd turn the light out and go to sleep pretty quick.

Fran scrunched down under her covers. "I have to get up early to meet Angie in town, so keep it quiet, okay?" Nine forty-five. Why wouldn't Fran shut up and go to sleep already!

I listened to her breathing get deeper and deeper. She'd always been a heavy sleeper, lucky for me. Usually her snoring bothered me. Sometimes I'd throw a pillow at her to make her wake up. But not tonight.

Nine fifty-five. It was now or never. I'd be late as it was. Would Jasper give up and go back to his camp?

I held my breath, hoping the floorboards wouldn't squeak under my feet, and got up. I piled all my books and papers beside the bed and stuck my pillow and some dirty clothes under the covers, more or less in the shape of a sleeping body, in case Fran woke up in the night. I turned off my light.

This is it, I thought. I felt my way around the bed and along the wall. I eased the door open. The hallway was dark and quiet. I tiptoed to the kitchen holding my breath. Still safe. If Pa or Fran woke up, I was just looking for a snack. I'd hardly eaten any dinner, after all.

Out the back door, across the yard to the barn. The moon glow was just showing over the hills. A night-hawk swooped over the back porch light, its whiskered beak scooping up mosquitoes. A bat winged past my head, almost brushing my hair. I startled sideways, edgy and nervous.

Rowdy caught my scent and trotted to the corral fence. "Good boy, Rowdy, it's just me," I whispered. He nickered softly, a whisper of his own.

I picked up a lead rope from the gatepost and clipped it to his halter, then led him to the barn. He stood nice and still while I threw on the saddle blanket, then the saddle. I pulled the cinch tight. He lowered his head to take the bit in his mouth. I'd never been so grateful to him. Some horses fought the bit and bloated up under the cinch. Not Rowdy.

First thing I checked when I lead him out of the barn was that the house was still dark. Yep, dark except for the porch light with its bugs and bats and nighthawks.

I put my foot in the stirrup, grabbed the saddle

horn, bounced up into the saddle. I wanted to shout, I was so scared and excited, riding out into the night like that to meet Jasper and rescue Glory. But I kept quiet and kept Rowdy calmed down to a walk until we were up the back road a way.

Halfway up the hill on the way to the Hanging Tree, I let Rowdy have his head and gallop up. The moon was peeking over the hills and the sage never smelled so sweet as in that cool night air. We slowed to a trot and then a walk as we crested the hill.

Jasper stood holding his dun pony's reins, peering into the darkness toward us. I could barely see him; he'd worn a black shirt and dark jeans, too.

I could see his teeth when he grinned though. "Hey, you made it! What, fifteen, twenty minutes late. I almost left, I got so nervous, but you made it!"

"Of course," I tried to sound confident, "why wouldn't I?"

"Oh I don't know . . . you could have gotten caught or chickened out." His voice sounded tight, more nervous than his words let on.

"Did you set up camp by the river?" I asked. "In case your folks go looking around."

"Yep. It's all good."

"Well then, mount up, Cowboy," I said, "let's do this."

Jasper swung up into the saddle. Tig and Rowdy both danced and sidestepped, their nostrils flared wide to the sharp night smells.

"To the rescue!" Jasper waved the black cowboy hat I'd given him like a starting flag.

Chapter 15

I felt bright as a comet, all fire and purpose and light. I turned Rowdy tight on his haunches, like we were running barrels, and headed down the hill in a long reaching lope. Jasper and Tig followed a few strides back.

We cantered down the crease between the hills and onto the old dirt road that wound toward the river. We followed the route we'd taken when we did our recon trip. The moon rose above the horizon as we moved along, and instead of getting darker, the world brightened around us.

We rode in silence mostly. I listened to the rocks crunching under the horses' hooves and the low hoot of a screech owl. The little brown bird flew along behind us for a while, perching in a juniper for a minute then flapping to catch up.

If we'd just been out for a ride, I'd have been happy and relaxed. As it was, my mind was racing ahead like a nervous colt.

When we'd been riding about half an hour, Jasper and Tig came up even with us on the road.

"You scared?" he asked.

"Yep," I answered. "Mostly excited now that we're actually doing it, though."

"Part of me's like, this is the best adventure ever, and part of me is really scared of getting caught."

"I know," I smiled at him, still trying to seem confident. "It's a good thing we're doing, though, saving a horse. I think even if we do get caught, it won't go too bad for us. Probably just have to give back the horse." I sounded sure, but I wasn't sure at all.

"Yeah," Jasper stroked his horse's neck under her mane. "We're too young to go to jail, and they don't hang horse thieves anymore, do they?"

"Everything will be fine, Jasper. Here's where we hid the horses last time." I eased Rowdy off the road and up the deer trail. We tied them there. I wished we'd been out a couple more times in the daylight. The place felt different in the dark.

I carried the halter and lead in one hand and stuck the wire cutters in my back pocket. Jasper had a plastic bag of carrots and gingersnaps mixed together, to lure Glory with.

"Let's go." I led the way back down the deer path. We passed the mailbox and climbed the gate across the drive. It was locked with a heavy chain and silver padlock. Hugging the fence line, we crept toward the house and barn.

"Momento!" Jasper called from behind. "My shirt's snagged."

I backed into the shadows closer to the fence while he freed his shirt from the rose bushes and caught up. Yellowish squares of light shone on two sides of the house.

"Looks like Mrs. McCarthy is a night owl. It must be close to eleven." I hadn't counted on her still being up. I couldn't see any vehicles in the dirt turn-around by the back door. That was a good sign.

I crouched down and whispered to Jasper, "Let's circle up on the hill behind the barn to get a better look. I want to be sure Carl's gone."

Jasper nodded.

When we were almost to the yard, another screech owl hooted and flapped out of the bushes ahead of us. I jumped and grabbed Jasper's arm. "Holy Moly!" We stood still for a full minute, until it had flown up to the top of a big locust tree in the yard. I lost it in the dark, but I felt like it was watching us.

We circled around the outer edge of the driveway to the hill and started up.

It was good and dark now. I was pretty sure someone scanning the hill from the house couldn't see us. Still, we edged up slowly, crouching and sometimes even crawling on our hands and knees. Rocks, sagebrush, more rocks, sand, tumbleweeds. Darkness, the moon hiding behind a cloud now. My heart *thump, thump, thumped* in my ears.

Halfway up the hill, Jasper yelped behind me. I turned back to shush him, and saw him sitting, holding his knee between his hands.

"Prickly pear," he breathed. I couldn't see the cactus spines in the darkness, but I had felt their stab before and knew how much they hurt.

"Hang on." I crawled over to him. I pulled the wire cutters out of my back pocket. I ran my hand over his knee, feeling for the spines. Before he could say anything, I gripped a spine with the pliers part of the wire cutters and jerked.

"Ay!" He startled backwards.

"Quiet!" I hissed at him. "Hold still." He did and I yanked two more spines out. I ran my hand over the knee of his jeans to make sure I'd gotten them all. "It'll be sore, but I think you'll live."

"Yeah, feels better already," I could see him smile his "good-sport" smile through the darkness. He crawled on up the hill ahead of me.

We stopped just short of the top. The barn, corral, woodshed, and house were darker blocks below. I thought I heard Glory snort in her pen, her nose sorting our smell from the night.

I scanned the buildings, figuring how far a run it would be from behind the barn to the corral. Jasper pulled at my sleeve. His eyes were wide as he pointed to the far side of the house.

I looked where he pointed and then blinked, trying to make it go away.

There, behind the house, out of sight from where we'd been on the ground, sat the flatbed truck. Carl McCarthy was sitting in the cab.

"Oh no!" I gasped, "he's here!"

Chapter 16

Maybe he's just leaving," Jasper whispered. We peered through the darkness at the truck parked behind the house.

We waited to hear the engine rev up. Nothing.

The truck door creaked open and Carl got out.

He walked to the corral and rested a foot on the bottom rail and watched Glory. She stayed on the far side, head low, her ears swiveled toward him. I wondered how much she sensed of his intent, and ours.

"Too bad you're just an old crow-bait nag," he said. "If you were a decent animal, I'd saddle you up and ride to Mexico."

A good five minutes passed before Carl crossed to the back porch and disappeared inside.

"Well, I sure was hoping he'd be gone," I said.

"Me too." Jasper's voice shook. "What are we going to do?"

"We'll start down as soon as they both go to bed," I whispered.

I rolled over on my back and let out a long breath. The sage smelled sharp but musty, and I caught a whiff of ozone in the air, kind of fresh and crackly, and knew that rain was coming in. *Good for covering our tracks*, I thought. Jasper lay back, too. It was like we were gathering strength.

After a bit, I sat up.

The kitchen light still shone a yellow square onto the dirt. The curtains made lacy shadows on the glass. Carl sat at the table, leaning forward. His voice came up the hill, loud and angry. We couldn't hear his words, but he sounded like he was drunk. The hair on my neck stood up.

After maybe half an hour or so, they finally got up from the table and left the room. Soon all the lights were out. I hoped they weren't insomniacs. We needed to get Glory out of here soon if I was going to make it home before sunrise.

We gave it a few minutes, then crept down the hill. I followed Jasper through the ragged humps of sage and black jumbles of rock. The moon rose in a bright sliver over the mountains to the east. The rain clouds I'd smelled huddled behind the hills to the south.

In the barnyard, I motioned Jasper toward the corral, while I watched from the deeper darkness of the barn doorway.

Glory threw her head up and snorted as Jasper slid off the top rail and into the corral. I held my breath. I could make out Jasper's shadow and the dark bulk of the horse like a shadow play; the horse coming near, then stepping away, Jasper's outstretched hand with a carrot held toward her nose.

Then I smelled the fresh earthy smell of the carrot as Glory's old teeth ground away at it. I heard Jasper gently pat her neck and his soft voice mumble to her.

The bolt on the corral gate squealed as Jasper drew it back, as if it hadn't been opened for some time. Jasper turned his head toward me, but I couldn't see his face under the dark brim of his hat. I could guess what his expression was though. My heart was racing.

I edged out of the shadows. Luckily, Glory stood quietly while I put the halter over her head. I rubbed her neck and whispered "Soooo, sooooo" in her ear as I buckled the cheek strap. Her soft lip searched my hand for more carrots.

"When we get out of here, girl," I said to her, "pretty

91

soon you'll have buckets of carrots, mountains of carrots." I pulled gently on the lead rope.

She didn't budge. "Come on, girl, please!" I pulled harder, released the tension and pulled again. She set her front feet and leaned back on her haunches.

"She's afraid," Jasper said, then he held out a carrot. She leaned forward and he moved it away from her. "Come on, come on," he pleaded with her.

I kept my eye on the house. This was the worst place to get stalled out, the easiest place to get caught.

Jasper let her have a bit of carrot and I eased her forward a step, then two; another few bites and she was through the gate. "Good girl," I said.

We headed straight for the driveway, the lead rope pulling taut between us. Glory followed slowly. Step. Step. Step. Each one thudding in my ears, the horse sounding as big and obvious as an elephant behind us. We had to get her out of sight.

I looked back once we got Glory moving down the driveway. I thought I saw the kitchen curtain pull back. Was that a face in the window or was I just imagining it?

We hurried her as fast as she would be hurried the rest of the way down the drive. I held my breath almost the entire way. Jasper walked on the other side, talking softly to her: "Good girl, easy girl, that's the way."

No sound came from the house. No door slamming open. No shouts of "Horse thieves!"

When we reached the locked gate at the bottom of the drive, I handed the lead rope to Jasper. "Hold her while I cut the fence."

As I reached for the wire cutters, I thought I heard something: a squeak, then a thud, like maybe the back door opening and slamming shut again.

Chapter 17

Did you hear that?" I asked Jasper, panic just around the bend. I stared at the house. It was still dark.

"Yep. Sounded like the back door. Do you think it's Carl?"

I didn't answer, but turned back to the task at hand. I fumbled with the wire cutters, dropping them twice in the dirt, feeling around in the dark, dry grass. Finally, shaky and looking over and over back toward the house, I went after the top wire.

Four strands of barbwire and one small pair of not-so-sharp wire cutters. It took me five minutes, maybe more, of twisting, prying, and cussing to cut the first two strands. I kept expecting to hear Carl's truck or footsteps or drunken voice shouting at us.

I paused to rest my hand, scared and frustrated. "Should have brought the bolt cutters and just taken that chain off the gate."

Jasper held Glory's rope. She stepped around and jerked her head back toward the house and barn. I looked where she looked but saw nothing, heard nothing but the night sounds; crickets, screech owl, *hoo-hooooo, hoo-hoooo*, far away, the coyotes wailing.

The bottom wire finally snapped free. I yanked the strands clear so Glory could step through.

Jasper held the lead rope right up under her chin, so she couldn't spook away. She stopped at the gap in the fence, not trusting it, not trusting us, yet. More sweet talk from Jasper. More carrots. *Please don't let Carl be there in the dark behind us,* I thought.

Glory finally stepped through in a quick trot. "Good girl," from Jasper and me, as if our mare had won the derby and not just passed this first little trial.

We hustled up the deer trail to the clearing where we'd left the other horses. Tig and Rowdy nickered and shuffled in the dark as we got closer.

"Ssshhhh . . . ssshhhhhh, eeeaasy," I whispered.

I leaped up into Rowdy's saddle and tied Glory's lead rope to my saddle horn. Rowdy backed a few steps, tightening the rope between him and Glory.

Jasper was up on Tig and hurried us all down the deer path. The coyotes yipped and barked on the far hills, urging us on.

At first, Glory tossed her head, jerking the rope. Rowdy ignored her and kept moving on steadily. She gradually settled in and kept stride with him.

The night was dead-dark now, except for the rising moon and a spattering of stars across the velvet sky. I couldn't hear the coyotes anymore over the pounding of the horses' hooves on the dirt road. I looked back over my shoulder again and again, but I didn't see anyone coming after us.

We made good time; down the road, through the first gate, up the draw, across the wheat field. The moon was only a sliver, but bright as polished silver.

Glory cantered alongside Rowdy, now and then jerking the rope tight, but mostly keeping up. She stumbled a bit on her overgrown hooves; I felt bad that she was probably hurting, but it couldn't be helped.

Jasper climbed down from the saddle to pull open another wire gate.

"You doing okay?" I asked, as Rowdy and Glory stepped through the gap.

"Yep," he said. "Pretty scary though. But I think we're going to make it!"

A trail along the creek emerged in front of us as a darker shadow.

"This way!" Rowdy and I plunged down the trail, into the tunnel of willows along the creek.

Branches reached out toward us, from both sides. Again and again I called out our signal for ducking: "Lay low, lay low."

Just when I started to breathe a little easier, I heard it; the steady growl of a motor coming from somewhere behind us.

"Aw, no!" Jasper breathed. I felt a lightning bolt of fear rush through me, from head to toe and back. A faint light flicked in and out of the brush about a half mile behind us. A truck couldn't have followed us this way. *Must be a four-wheeler,* I thought.

My stomach did a somersault like I was going to throw up. I kicked Rowdy into a canter and Glory's rope pulled taut between us. We raced off into the darkness, Jasper and Tig behind us somewhere.

If there was a four-wheeler on this trail at night, it could only be coming for us. It could only be Carl McCarthy.

Chapter 18

Hiding from some crazy guy on a four-wheeler would have been easy enough on foot. The machines roared like a mad bull and crashed through brush like a herd of buffalo. On foot, I could have dodged into a ditch or rock cleft and been invisible while he charged by. Getting away with three horses, however, was a lot trickier.

I waited a long minute for Jasper and Tig to catch up, wanting to make a quick plan. Rowdy and Glory pranced and snorted. They heard the engine, too. Still no sign of Jasper. Where in the world was he?

The headlights bounced closer.

Another minute ticked by and still no Jasper. I wheeled Rowdy on his haunches. Glory followed in a tight circle. We'd have to go on without them. If we waited any longer we'd be caught. I hoped Jasper was okay, maybe hiding somewhere, and would meet up with us at the ranch.

I was trying to get the horses going forward again when something strange happened. The headlights behind us veered off the trail and blinked out of sight.

The lights reappeared on the sloping field off to our left. Did Carl think we'd headed up the hill? The engine growl grew quieter as the machine moved farther away.

Hooray! We'd lost him!

Then, I saw what had lured our pursuer; Jasper and Tig stood silhouetted on the hilltop, like a statue of some war hero on his faithful mount, poised, courageous, invincible.

The four-wheeler roared across the open field toward them.

My heart jumped into my throat. Jasper was playing the bait, leading Carl away from us. But what would happen if Carl caught up to him? Jasper was sacrificing himself to save us. Would I have done the same?

As I watched, my friend and his horse dropped over the far side of the hill and left the moonlight shining down on emptiness.

"Yeah!" I said to the horses, a huge grin spread across my face, and we were off again.

I had to push my worry about Jasper and Tig out of my head as I urged Rowdy and Glory forward. Another half mile or so on the creek path and the trees thinned out.

We broke out of the creek brush and into the east field of the Owens Ranch. A half-dozen mule deer startled from under the gnarled apple trees and jumped the zigzagging split rail and were gone up the hill.

The owl swooped down over us as we trotted, all breathing hard, into the barnyard. I jumped down and gave Rowdy a kiss between his flaring nostrils.

"You were fast as lightning!" I told my horse. "We couldn't have done it without you."

I turned to Glory. She was huffing and her head hung down.

"Poor old girl." I rubbed her neck until she picked her head up and nuzzled my hand. "You can rest up now. You did real good, too."

The moon shone down on the barnyard like a blessing, lighting the pile of junk we'd cleaned out of the barn, the corral rails we'd repaired.

I led Glory into the barn and found her stall by feel: the floorboards under my feet, the wood of the walls under my fingertips. I was glad we'd cleaned all the junk out—nothing to trip on now.

The owl flapped silently onto the windowsill and swiveled her head at me as I unhooked the lead rope from Glory's halter and shut the stall door behind her thin rump.

In the dark, I heard Glory snuffle and rustle as she found her hay and started eating. I sat down on a bale and leaned against the wall. After a few minutes, she noisily sucked up a long draft of water and went back to eating her hay.

I looked out the little square window in the barn wall. Rowdy grazed on the weedy remains of the lawn around the fallen porch. The house and chicken coop stood dark and silent. Where was Jasper? Had Carl caught him?

Was Carl coming for me right now?

I shook out a dusty burlap bag and rubbed Glory's sides and back. When the sweat was mostly dry, I brushed her all over. She leaned against me. She let me pick up each overgrown hoof and pick out bits of gravel. Who would we find to trim her hooves?

I ran my fingers through her tangled mane and tail. All through it, she just kept eating. Smoothing my palm over her bony ribs, I felt a surge of relief that she was safe now. At least I hoped so.

"You're gonna be all right, girl," I said as I stroked

her neck. "You'll put some weight on these bones and start to feel better real soon."

Outside, Rowdy snorted and Glory jerked her head up.

Oh, please let that be Jasper.

Chapter 19

I stood at the tiny barn window and peeked out. A bulky shadow crouched quick and low between the farmhouse and the pump house. Too big to be Jasper, and he wouldn't be sneaking. Suddenly, the shadow dashed across the moonlit barnyard and ducked behind the corral gate. Carl.

I backed into the dark depths of the barn and sorted through my options as quickly as I could: I could hide or I could run.

And then there was Glory. She'd caught Carl's scent. She stamped and snorted in her stall.

I couldn't let Carl just waltz in and take her back, not after everything we'd done to keep her safe. Not when I knew what would happen if he got hold of her.

I grabbed the halter from the nail where Jasper had

hung it earlier in the week, eased back the bolt on the stall door, and slipped in next to Glory. She was quivering, her skin hot and twitching, as she danced in place, her eyes on the barn door. I thought I could smell him, too, all rank and fierce, like a bear.

"Easy, girl," I breathed into her ear as I buckled the halter. I led her from the stall into the open hallway of the barn and up-ended an empty apple crate to stand on. I grabbed a handful of mane and swung up.

Squeezing my legs tight around her sides sent her bounding for the open barn door and the black night beyond.

I'd had a vision of galloping off into the night, clinging low and tight on Glory's back, her mane streaming in my face, her hooves flying over the dark earth.

Instead, we took two strides out the barn door before Carl stepped from the shadows and grabbed the lead rope. I swear he let out a roar, like an ogre, as he yanked hard, wheeling Glory and me to face him.

"Let go!" I shouted, hitting at him with the end of the lead rope.

"Horse thief!" Carl grabbed at my leg but I yanked it out of his reach. "I'll crush you, girl! Takin' my property, you got no right to that animal!"

"You don't care about Glory," I yelled back at him.

"You starve her and now you're gonna have her killed, just for a few bucks."

Glory threw her head up and backed up quick, her eyes wild and rimmed in white. Flinging her head, she jerked the lead rope from Carl's hand.

"OOOOWWWWW!" Carl cradled one hand in the other, a red rope burn cut across his palm. He swore a blue streak. Before we could get away, he grabbed at the rope with his good hand.

I clung to Glory's neck as she reared up quick on her haunches. She jabbed out with her front hooves, one-two, like one of those trained battle horses I'd read about, the ones who fought alongside the knights.

A hoof caught Carl on the side of the head. I heard it hit like a slab of meat slammed down a butcher's table. He collapsed in the dirt. I went down, too, slipping sideways and nearly under Glory's front feet as she crashed down.

I lay on my back, arms covering my face, knees drawn up, Glory's hooves churning up dust around me.

I peeked through my arms at her belly, felt her hooves graze my shoulders and legs as she straddled me.

I took a chance and rolled to my left, out from under the horse.

The clouds had parted and silver light shone down on our chaotic triangle in the barnyard. I could see Glory trembling in the moonlight. Carl was crawling slowly to his feet, blood running down the side of his face. And I saw myself there, as if from high up, filthy, shivering with fear and anger, pulling myself up with a hand on the fence rail.

I shook my head clear, then dodged into the shadow between the barn and coop. When I looked back, Glory was nowhere in sight. And just like that, everything we'd worked for, probably risked our lives for, was gone.

My heart ached. "Oh, Glory," I whispered, "Glory, please come back."

Chapter 20

I heard Carl hawking something up onto the dirt and groaning.

Good, I thought, *I hope you're hurt bad*.

I felt my way along the chicken coop, its ragged whitewash scabbing off under my fingers. I slipped in the door of the coop and shut it behind me. I was safe for the moment. I was inside and Carl was outside.

Then I realized my mistake: I was trapped! If Carl came through that door after me, I'd have no way out.

I felt my way along the wall by the door until I reached a corner. Then I inched along the back wall until I ran into a bank of nesting boxes nailed to the wall, each one bristly with a tangled nest of straw. Another corner, another wall, another corner and then back to the door. No way out.

Cobwebs clung to my face and hands. Dried chicken manure stunk under my feet. Mice squeaked and skittered into even darker holes.

Heavy steps shuffled outside, nearing the coop.

An idea flashed in my mind then. The coop had a pen attached to one side. The chickens had to get out into the pen somehow. There must be an opening somewhere in the wall. Probably lower down than I'd looked before.

I dropped to my hands and knees in the ancient chicken manure. I ran my hands along the bottom boards of the wall. It had to be here somewhere. Something furry skittered under my arm and I stifled a yelp.

Finally, I found it: a ragged square cut into the planks. I heard the coop door bang open behind me, so I launched myself at the hole.

Good thing I'm skinny. Any bigger and I'd have gotten stuck for sure. As it was, I had to wriggle to get my shoulders through.

"I've got you now, you little thief!" Carl growled behind me.

His boots pounded across the floorboards. My head and body were out in the pen when I felt his hand grab my ankle.

Carl tightened his fingers, but I kicked hard and he lost his grip for a second. I wriggled farther out. He grabbed me again and jerked me back toward him, scraping my thighs against the edge of the hole.

"Let go of me!" I screamed and kicked harder. This time my boot hit something. I heard a loud "OOF!" and he dropped my leg.

I wriggled harder and slipped out onto the ground below the coop. I was free.

I ran about three steps and crashed into the chicken wire around the pen. Carl swore behind me as he tried to get his big body through the hole. Only his head and one arm stuck out, flailing at me. It would have been funny in another place and time. But I knew Carl wouldn't stay stuck in that chicken coop for long. I had to get out of here.

I scrambled around, running my hands over the fence until I found a gap where two pieces of chicken wire had separated. I pulled myself through, the wire scratching my face and arms and catching at my shirt.

I spotted a little building down by the creek—must have been the old pump house. I hadn't noticed it before, half covered in overgrown wild roses and willow. I made leaping bounds through waist-high grass to get to it, my heart and lungs aching. I didn't look back.

Behind the pump house, I rested a minute, my hands on my thighs, my head down. How in the world had it gotten to this? And where was Jasper? I hoped Carl hadn't caught up to him. But I couldn't afford to think like that right now.

I heard dry boards cracking nearby. I peeked out to see Carl's dark hulk stumbling over a pile of rotting planks stacked between the coop and the pump house. At least he was a poor sneak.

He reeled from the head wound where Glory had kicked him, and he moved toward me in a crooked lurch. I swear his eyes lit up red in the moonlight, as he got nearer.

I was as blame tired as I'd ever been, but I pushed myself off and made for the creek. I could hear water tumbling over the rocks below me. In the movies, the guy being chased always loses his chasers by running through the water. Maybe it would work for me, too.

I made it about three steps down the bank before I fell. The toe of my boot caught under something and down I went. I fell hard and I guess my head must've hit a rock. I don't remember. I just fell and then dove into blackness.

Chapter 21

When I opened my eyes, my head throbbed. Thin moonlight striped the wooden floor beneath me.

Where was I?

I looked around and discovered the light was leaking between warped boards of the walls. I was back in the barn.

I remembered running in the dark. Something behind me. Fear. Falling. I closed my eyes again. My head really hurt. Must have hit it on something.

I thought hard and my memories spun, but slowly it came back to me: rescuing Glory, Jasper and Tig on the hilltop, Carl chasing me, and Glory gone! All this for nothing.

I heard a ragged breath to my right. Carl's sleeping

bulk slouched in an old lawn chair. His mouth drooped wide showing yellow teeth beneath his moustache.

My wrists hurt. I looked down and found them bound tight in front of me with baling twine. The twine was lashed to a post. I moved my hands slowly up to where my head hurt. I felt a sticky mat of hair and a ragged ridge in my scalp: a tear in the skin crusted over with dried blood.

How had it all gone so wrong when we were trying to do something right?

I went over it in my head, fast motion, all I could remember about the night. Maybe we should have waited longer before we took Glory from the corral. Maybe we picked the wrong night. Maybe I should have asked Pa for help with Glory instead of stealing her.

No use thinking about that now, I argued with myself, what's done is done. So I turned my thoughts to my captor instead. What had turned Carl so sour? He'd grown up with Pa, gone to school with him, too. How'd they turn out so different? Carl had quit school and now he was a drunk bully who picked on his mom and on a defenseless horse. Pa had finished school, had a wife and a family, owned his own ranch and made a good living.

Coincidence? I wondered. Maybe, maybe not.

As I rolled over to spit dirt out of my dry mouth, I caught a movement at the barn door. Jasper's black hat and dirty face peeked in and I smiled in quick relief. He raised a finger to his lips and his wide eyes darted between me and sleeping Carl.

I hoped Jasper had a plan, because my own thoughts jumbled up and split apart before I could get them in any kind of order. Had we saved Glory or just doomed ourselves?

Dirt turned to mud in my mouth. My torn scalp throbbed and ached with my pulse: one-two, one-two, one-two. The doorway gaped empty again.

Where had Jasper gone? To get help? I closed my eyes, hoping to calm the throbbing in my head.

When I opened my eyes again, Jasper was back at the door, a snake of rope coiled in his hand. He held it easy, natural. It was his calf-roping lariat, the one that he kept tied to his saddle.

My first thought was, *No way, don't try it!* My second was, *Could it work?* And my third, as Jasper swung a loop through the still barn air was, *God, let it land true and snug up fast.*

What happened was somewhere in-between. The rope fell true enough, settling around Carl and the chair back. Jasper jerked it tight, which was more difficult and slower on foot than from horseback. He planted his feet and strained at the rope. Carl was pulled tight to the chair.

He awoke with a roar and jerked himself over sideways. Jasper raced over to me, skidding to my side. His pocketknife was out in a flash and he sawed through the twine at my wrists in a matter of seconds.

I jumped up and grabbed the lariat's free end as Carl was struggling to get the loop over his head. I jerked the rope tight and snaked it around the post I'd been tied to.

I braced my foot on the post and pulled hard. Carl and the chair pulled up tight against the post. Carl shouted and swore as I wound the rope tight around his chest, pinning his arms to his sides.

Jasper grabbed the rope just up from where I held it. The bristly stiffness bit and burned my hands as we yanked it tighter. I could feel the anger rippling off our prisoner like fire. My hands shook as I snugged and knotted the rope. Jasper bound Carl's feet with baling twine, tied him neat as a thrown calf.

He raged at us like a wounded bear. "They hang horse thieves! You bet they do!" Carl roared. "You two are gonna be hangin' side by side. Swingin' in the wind!" Spit flew from his mouth as he hollered at us.

"Shut up!" I yelled back at him. I grabbed a rat-chewed gunnysack and crammed the end of it in his mouth. I couldn't stand to hear another word.

The silence was a blessing. Relief and fear shivered back and forth between Jasper and me. Cold sweat dripped down my forehead. Jasper shone like a frightened angel in the moonlight cutting through the rafters.

"Let's get out of here," I said, taking one last look at Carl. Even hog-tied and gagged, he still scared me.

"Where's Glory?" Jasper asked as we jogged to Tig and Rowdy.

"Oh, Jas!" I couldn't even look at him. He'd risked his life for Glory and now she was gone. I held Rowdy's reins, slipped my foot into the stirrup, and swung up.

"Carl came after us, so I tried to ride away on her. But then I fell and Glory was so brave. She knocked him down and ran off." I wiped tears from my filthy face with my sleeve.

Jasper had Tig by the reins. "It's okay," he said calmly, "we'll find her. She's probably eating that nice tall grass in the orchard." He mounted up.

"Yeah, maybe. I hope so." I tried to muster up his optimism. "You were great, Jasper. You saved my life. You could have just got away yourself, but you came back. And it was so cool the way you roped Carl like that.

I never knew you had this secret hero side." I said it kind of joking, but I wasn't.

He lowered his eyes, but smiled a little. "No era nada," he said; it was nothing. "Just like roping a calf. A big fat calf!" He grinned some of the fear off his face.

We turned the horses toward the orchard. Might as well look for Glory as we headed home. We heard it at the same time; the grind of an engine, maybe a quarter mile up the road from us, cut the air. Someone was coming fast up the driveway.

I thought to myself, *This is the part where the outlaws give up, where the posse charges in, and the horse thieves know they're beat. All exits cut off: dead-end canyons, sheer cliffs, uncrossable rivers. No way out.*

That was us.

Chapter 22

A white SUV with COUNTY SHERIFF on the door skidded to a stop in the barnyard. Rowdy and Tig danced in the headlights, blinking and snorting.

My heart double-bumped. Part of me, the outlaw part, wanted to turn to Jasper and holler, "Go! Go! Go!" and make a run for it. But I kept quiet. They knew who we were. Where exactly could we go now?

Jasper and I pulled the horses to a stop. We locked eyes for a minute, then slowly raised our hands in the air.

A couple more pickup trucks pulled in behind the sheriff. One was Pa's. The other was Danny's. I could see Jasper's parents sitting next to Jasper's brother in the cab. I felt sick to my stomach.

Sheriff Gonzales got out of one side of the SUV, and Deputy Kim got out of the other. They both stood, hands on hips, surveying the barnyard. The sheriff rested his hand on his gun as he looked up at Jasper and then at me. "Get down off those horses," he said.

We both kicked a leg over the saddle and slid down. We stood looking at the dirt, our hands still held high.

Everyone was out of the trucks now; Pa and Fran, Jasper's mom and dad, all lit by the glare of the headlights, staring at us.

Danny stood just behind the sheriff. I glared at him.

"I had to tell," Danny said. "I went by your camping spot and you guys weren't there. I was afraid you'd get hurt running around out here in the dark with that crazy Carl."

I shook my head. He'd betrayed us.

"So who wants to tell me what's going on here?" the sheriff said, squinting at us from under his hat brim.

"I . . . I . . . well, we . . ." Jasper couldn't shake the words out.

I looked up at the sheriff, but avoided Pa's glaring eyes. "We, Jasper and me, we rescued a horse. I mean, I guess we kind of stole her. But we had to."

Sheriff Gonzales nodded to the deputy, who walked away toward the corral. Then he squinted his eyes even narrower. I was surprised he could even see us. "You two stole a horse. That's a very serious crime. What do you mean 'We had to'?"

"She was starving," I said, "weak, overgrown hooves, she looked like a skeleton."

Jasper found his voice. "He was gonna take her to the auction. Glory would've been killed. She didn't deserve that. We were gonna take care of her."

"Who was going to take her to the auction?" the sheriff asked. "Whose horse did you steal?"

Just then, Deputy Kim hollered from the doorway of the barn: "Sheriff, there's a guy tied up in here."

"Wait right here." Sheriff Gonzales stared hard at me, then at Jasper. "Don't move a muscle."

Pa stepped up. "Don't worry, they won't."

The sheriff drew his gun from its holster and walked into the barn.

When I looked up, Pa's face glared red in the bright headlights. I'd never seen him so mad.

"I'm sorry, Pa," I looked back at the ground, "we didn't know what else to do. I felt so bad for her."

Pa just shook his head, like he couldn't trust himself to talk. His neck muscles were tight. He ran his fingers through his hair and shook his head again.

"We just wanted to help." I whispered the last part because I was choking back tears now.

The sheriff's voice interrupted us: "Get up!" We all turned toward the barn.

A minute later, Kim and Sheriff Gonzales emerged pushing Carl ahead of them. Carl was handcuffed, his arms pulled back behind him.

He looked a sorry sight, but I guess we did, too, all of us torn and dirty and wrung-out. He glared at us and spit from under his big moustache.

Kim pushed Carl's head down, eased him into the back of the SUV, and shut the door. Jasper and I watched, our mouths hanging open. Here was the guy who'd chased us half the night, maybe even would have killed us over one bony old horse. And now they were hauling him off to jail, not us!

"You can put your hands down, kids," the sheriff said when he got back to us. "Turns out you're heroes after all."

He pushed his hat back and his eyes looked wider and friendlier. "You've managed to catch a real criminal. We've been looking for Carl McCarthy for weeks. There's a warrant out for his arrest for a couple of armed robberies over in the valley."

Jasper's face lit up and I grinned back at him. Seemed like our luck might be changing.

Pa looked surprised and kind of relieved.

Fran uncrossed her arms and ran over to me. "Stupid!" she said as she hugged me. "You really scared us!" She pushed the hair away from the gash on my head. "We better get that cleaned up. Might even need stitches."

Jasper's mother hugged him as well. "Niño, why didn't you ask us for help with the horse?" His father nodded.

"I didn't think you would," Jasper answered. "You won't even let me have a dog. I sure didn't think you'd let me have a horse. Especially one we had to steal."

Finally, Pa walked over and wrapped an arm around me. "I'm so glad you're safe, Cass. If anything had happened to you, I don't know . . ." He shook his head and squeezed my shoulder. "But you made some really bad decisions tonight. You know that, don't you?"

"I do," I whispered. "I've been making a lot of bad decisions lately." I felt a new wave of determination welling up in me. "But tonight I realized I don't want to be like Carl. I want to be like you, Pa. I'm going to do better in school. Starting Monday."

"That's really good to hear, Cassie. But you're still grounded." He smiled at me as he said it, though, which made it a little easier to hear.

"You're grounded too, Jasper," said his father. Jasper just smiled. I think he wasn't going to mind being safe at home for a while.

"So where *is* this horse that caused all this trouble?" Sheriff Gonzales looked around. The barnyard was getting light now as the sun began to rise over the hills. It was morning. It felt like we'd been on our adventure for days, not just overnight.

"Glory ran off." I lowered my head, not feeling too heroic anymore. "I don't know where she is now." I felt a tear slip down my dirty face as I scanned the orchard for the horse I'd already come to love. No Glory.

"Maybe she'll turn up," Pa said.

All at once, my legs felt like jelly, and my head began pounding like a bass drum. I let out a groan.

"Let's get you home, Cass." Pa steered me toward our truck where Fran was leaning close to Danny, whispering and smiling.

"That was a brave thing you did tonight, Cass," Pa said as he helped me into the truck. "Stupid, but brave. You've got a good heart—just like your mom. I'm proud of you." He kissed my forehead and closed the door.

I slumped against Fran's shoulder and was sound asleep before we were halfway home.

Epilogue

Here's the long and the short of it: a lot of things changed. Carl McCarthy went to jail for robbing a bunch of homes over in the valley. We wouldn't be seeing him again for a long, long time. At least I hoped not.

And I started working hard on my schoolwork. I even got a head start on the eighth-grade reading list. Ms. T. didn't have to call Pa again.

Glory wandered back to her ranch on her own the very next day. Lucky for us, Mrs. McCarthy didn't press charges for the horse thieving. She hadn't wanted Glory to end up at the glue factory any more than we had.

Even though Pa'd said he was proud of me, he still had to punish me for breaking the law, and his rules. Jasper's parents agreed with my pa that we should help

Mrs. McCarthy on her ranch to make up for stealing her horse.

So, I was pretty much grounded for the rest of the school year and most of the summer, except for going to Mrs. McCarthy's with Jasper. We shoveled out her barns, threw hay to her cows, pulled weeds out of her vegetable garden, mowed her yard—whatever needed doing. We went every weekend and twice during the week . . . *forever*.

At first, I thought about all the other things we could be doing with our time: camping, riding, swimming. But that changed, too. After a couple of weeks, I actually started looking forward to helping out.

I especially liked taking care of Glory. That was no punishment at all. Before long, she nickered whenever she saw Jasper and me ride up.

Pa called the farrier to trim her hooves. He paid for half and Jasper and I paid the other half. After that, Glory felt good enough to trot around the grassy pasture we'd helped fence, tossing her head and flicking her tail. Jasper and I would sit and watch her, feeling good that we'd actually rescued her, after all.

Even Mrs. McCarthy changed. She didn't seem so sad. Some days she stood at her window and watched us groom Glory. I'd wave the currycomb at her and she'd wave back and smile. And some days, she'd invite Jasper and me into the kitchen, behind the lace curtains, and give us hot gingerbread straight from the oven.

But what changed the most was me and Jas. After the rescue, the next time we got on the school bus, all the rowdy, obnoxious kids hushed and stared openmouthed at us. And the kids in my classes stopped snickering whenever I opened my mouth. Overnight, we'd become heroes for our crime.

More important, though, was that we'd done the right thing. I knew it in my heart every time I looked at Glory.

Glossary of Horse Terms

Bit: The part of the bridle that fits in the horse's mouth, usually a metal bar, but sometimes rubber. It is held on by the cheek straps of the head stall.

Bridle: A set of straps that fits around the horse's head to hold the bit and reins in place; used for directing the horse.

Canter: A three-beat forward movement, usually faster than a trot; called a lope in western riding terms.

Cinch: A flat strap that passes under the horse's belly to secure the saddle to the animal's back.

Dun: Yellowish or tan coat with a darker-colored mane and tail, a dark stripe along the back, and occasionally faint leg stripes and a possible stripe across the withers (shoulder).

Gait: The pattern of movement of the horse's legs and hoof-falls on the ground. The natural gaits are the walk, trot, canter (or lope), and gallop.

Gallop: The fastest natural horse gait after the canter. In the gallop, all four hooves are off the ground at one time.

Gelding: A castrated male horse (made unable to sire offspring).

Groom: To clean and brush a horse, including picking dirt and rocks from hooves, combing the mane and tail, and removing dust and dirt from the coat.

Halter: A rope, nylon, or leather device that fits around the horse's head. A lead rope is attached, usually to a ring under the chin to lead or tie the animal.

Mare: A mature female horse.

Paint: A western stock horse with a pattern of white and dark coat colors. A breed developed from spotted horses with Quarter Horse and Thoroughbred bloodlines.

Pony: A breed of horse that measures 14.2 "hands" or less. A hand is equal to four inches.

Rein: A long strap attached to the bridle that is held by the rider to guide the horse; used in pairs, one on each side of the neck.

Saddle: The equipment strapped to the horse's back where the rider sits. A western saddle has a "horn" in front, sometimes used to tie a rope to when working with cattle, and a cantle behind the rider to make sitting more stable and comfortable.

Stirrups: U-shaped supports for the rider's foot, attached to the saddle with stirrup leathers and used to help mount the horse and to aid in balance when riding.

Tack: The equipment that horses wear including saddle, bridle, saddle blanket, halter, etc.

Trot: A diagonal two-beat horse gait.

Cassie and Jasper to the Rescue
Study Guide Questions

1. Cassie and Jasper grew up around ranch animals. How might kids living in the country think about or treat animals differently from city kids?

2. If an animal was hurt or in trouble and no one else was helping, what would you do?

3. The kids in the book broke the law when they took Glory. Is it ever okay to commit a crime? Would you have taken Glory?

4. Sometimes fear gets in the way of doing what we want or what we think is right. How did Jasper get past his fears?

5. Do you think that either Jasper or Cassie would have rescued Glory on his or her own? Why or why not? What would have been different?

6. Have you ever done something out of compassion, even though other people thought it was wrong? Would you do it again?

CPSIA information can be obtained at www.ICGtesting.com
Printed in the USA
BVOW05s1105100414

349874BV00003B/3/P